Mattie was going to bolt.

David needed to do some fast talking if he wanted her to stay, or his story would be dead before it even began. "The prize money is the same, you know. *And* you don't have to eat bugs. Fifty thousand to the Average Jill just for suffering through all the dates and then a hundred-thousand-dollar purse for her to split if she falls in love and gets engaged at the end."

Mattie's eyes grew wide. For a second, David had to remember to breathe. It wasn't fair that one woman should have eyes that captivating. "With who?"

"With me, of course."

"You?"

He cleared his throat. Whoa. That hadn't come out as he'd intended. In fact, he hadn't even wanted it to come out. Besides, he wasn't here to fall in love. He wanted the story—not the girl.

Didn't he?

D0012610

Dear Reader,

What is the best gift you ever received? Chances are it came from a loved one and reflects to some degree the love you share. Or maybe the gift was something like a cruise or a trip to an exotic locale that raised the hope of finding romance and lasting love. Well, it's no different for this month's heroes and heroines, who will all receive special gifts that extend beyond the holiday season to provide a lifetime of happiness.

Karen Rose Smith starts off this month's offerings with *Twelfth Night Proposal* (#1794)—the final installment in the SHAKESPEARE IN LOVE continuity. Set during the holidays, the hero's love enables the plain-Jane heroine to become the glowing beauty she was always meant to be. In *The Dating Game* (#1795) by Shirley Jump, a package delivered to the wrong address lands the heroine on a reality dating show. Julianna Morris writes a memorable romance with *Meet Me under the Mistletoe* (#1796), in which the heroine ends up giving a widower the son he "lost" when his mother died. Finally, in Donna Clayton's stirring romance *Bound by Honor* (#1797), the heroine receives a "life present" when she saves the Native American hero's life.

When you're drawing up your New Year's resolutions, be sure to put reading Silhouette Romance right at the top. After all, it's the love these heroines discover that reminds us all of what truly matters most in life.

With all best wishes for the holidays and a happy and healthy 2006.

Ann Leslie Tuttle
Associate Senior Editor

Please address questions and book requests to:
Silhouette Reader Service
U.S.: 3010 Walden Ave., P.O. Box 1325, Buffalo, NY 14269
Canadian: P.O. Box 609, Fort Erie, Ont. L2A 5X3

SHIRLEY JUMP

The Dating Game

SILHOUETTE **Romance**®

Published by Silhouette Books

America's Publisher of Contemporary Romance

If you purchased this book without a cover you should be aware
that this book is stolen property. It was reported as "unsold and
destroyed" to the publisher, and neither the author nor the
publisher has received any payment for this "stripped book."

To my husband, who almost went to the wrong address on our first date,
and who stole my heart through letters and packages. If we'd have been
smart, honey, we'd have bought stock in FedEx and UPS when we met.

For my daughter, who knows her mother has the athletic ability of a
goldfish, and coached me through the soccer scenes without laughing.
Finally, to all the young female athletes, who work and play hard.
The boys certainly have something to contend with
when the girls are on the field. Girls rock!

SILHOUETTE BOOKS

RECYCLED PAPER

ISBN 0-373-19795-0

THE DATING GAME

Copyright © 2005 by Shirley Kawa-Jump

All rights reserved. Except for use in any review, the reproduction
or utilization of this work in whole or in part in any form by any
electronic, mechanical or other means, now known or hereafter
invented, including xerography, photocopying and recording, or in
any information storage or retrieval system, is forbidden without
the written permission of the editorial office, Silhouette Books,
233 Broadway, New York, NY 10279 U.S.A.

All characters in this book have no existence outside the imagination of
the author and have no relation whatsoever to anyone bearing the same
name or names. They are not even distantly inspired by any individual
known or unknown to the author, and all incidents are pure invention.

This edition published by arrangement with Harlequin Books S.A.

® and TM are trademarks of Harlequin Books S.A., used under license.
Trademarks indicated with ® are registered in the United States Patent
and Trademark Office, the Canadian Trade Marks Office and in other
countries.

Visit Silhouette Books at www.eHarlequin.com

Printed in U.S.A.

Books by Shirley Jump

Silhouette Romance

The Virgin's Proposal #1641
The Bachelor's Dare #1700
The Daddy's Promise #1724
Her Frog Prince #1746
Kissed by Cat #1757
The Marine's Kiss #1781
The Dating Game #1795

*The Dole Family

SHIRLEY JUMP

spends her days writing romantic comedies with sweet attitude to feed her shoe addiction and avoid housework. A wife and mother of two, her real life helps her maintain her sense of humor. She swears that if she didn't laugh, she'd be fatally overcome by things like uncooperative llamas at birthday parties and chipmunks in the bathroom. When she isn't writing, Shirley's either eating or shopping. Or on a really good day, doing both at the same time.

Her first novel for Silhouette, *The Virgin's Proposal,* won the Bookseller's Best Award in 2004. Though she framed the award, it didn't impress the kids enough to make them do the dishes more often. In fact, life as a published author is pretty much like life as it was before, except now Shirley conveniently pulls a deadline out of thin air whenever the laundry piles up.

Read excerpts, see reviews or learn more about Shirley at www.shirleyjump.com.

Dear Reader,

Did you ever get the wrong package delivered to your house? What if that wrong package had been delivered on purpose, and it could lead to finding your true love? That's where this book begins, with matchmaker and deliveryman Bowden Hartman taking love matters into his own hands.

He sets his sights on Mattie Grant, a soccer coach who has everything *but* love on her mind when she signs up for a reality survival show. Bowden has other plans for her, though, and sends her to a completely different show—a dating game that's about to change her life and that of jaded reporter-turned-bachelor David Bennett.

The story just proves one thing—you never know when that package might lead you to love!

Prologue

On Monday morning Bowden Hartman toyed with the envelope in his hands and considered breaking every rule that went with the hideous olive-green uniform he wore. Well, not *every* rule. Just a couple of the more important ones.

The front of the envelope made no bones about his mission. "Overnight delivery, by 10:00 a.m.," blared the red banner. A quick, on-time delivery—his specialty, and what they paid him to do every day at Speedy Delivery Services.

Okay, he'd make the overnight delivery. Just not *this* letter to *this* person.

He knew better than to mess with the packages, of

course. But when had he ever followed the rules, rather than what his instincts told him was right?

Not very often. That was, indeed, what made his life fun and kept this job from being unbearable.

He didn't *need* to work—not since he'd inherited the rest of the Hartman fortune. But since his father's death two years ago, Bowden had found he *liked* to work, especially jobs where people were glad to see him and he got to indulge his bad habit of meddling in other people's lives.

Especially their love lives. If there was anything Bowden Hartman liked to see, it was a happy ending.

"You got lucky, Hartman," one of his co-workers, Jimmy Landry, said from across the room, hoisting a coffee mug in tribute. "What I wouldn't give to be delivering *that* letter today."

"Which one?"

"The one to the hot woman who's going to be on the *Love and the Average Jill* reality show. I heard they got the former Miss Indiana. Bet she gives you a kiss for bringing that by." Jimmy flipped him a thumbs-up. "I know I'll be tuning in every night to see that girl, er, show."

Bowden glanced again at the envelope in his palm. It was, as he already knew, addressed to Tiffany Barrett, Miss Indiana of two years ago. Across from him sat stacks of other envelopes meant for the rest of that show's and another show's contestants, many of which were in the pile for his route. Some were going to the bachelors who'd been chosen to go on the show with her and compete for the "average" Jill, the newest star in Lawford, Indiana's, Channel Ten nightly seven-o'clock lineup. Other letters were designated for the outdoors-loving competitors of *Survival of the Fittest,* the second reality show Lawford Channel Ten was debuting this week.

The executive producer of the show had come in himself at five yesterday, handed over the envelopes, noting which ones were for chosen contestants on each show—and therefore had to be delivered, and which ones were for the rejects. He'd also given everyone explicit directions not to peek at or leak the information, or he'd have their heads on a platter.

Well, he hadn't actually said "heads" or mentioned "platter." He'd used other—and worse—potential consequences for leaking the news. The other men in the office had steered clear of the envelopes, guarding all protruding body parts that might come anywhere near the piles.

Bowden hadn't said a word but hadn't followed the producer's demands, either. He'd peeked. He'd then been up half the night concocting a plan.

Bowden picked up another letter slated for his route, this one for *Survival of the Fittest.* Part of a big blitz, the producer had said, to up the ratings for the local TV station by debuting two knock-off reality shows the same week.

This letter was marked for Mattie Grant, who lived in the historic Pierpont Apartments downtown, one of the first stops on Bowden's route. A nice woman, though in need of a change. He'd met her several times over the year he'd worked here, when he'd delivered special cleats or a shipment of customized shirts for the young girls' soccer league she coached.

They'd chatted for a few minutes last week while he'd dropped off her latest delivery. She'd let it slip that she'd auditioned for the survival show. In his hand, he knew, was her letter telling her she'd been accepted as one of the contestants.

He weighed the two letters, one in each palm, Mattie's against the one for Miss Indiana. The idea he'd had last night returned. He shouldn't. If he ever got caught, it would be a sure way to get fired.

Ah, to hell with the consequences. Bowden Hartman believed firmly that breaking the rules was a whole lot more fun than following them.

Chapter One

Mattie Grant was prepared for anything. Mosquitoes the size of hummingbirds. Fires with all the durability of tissues, drinking water with enough germs to contaminate a small rodent colony.

She could handle all of it. And win.

She had, after all, trained for competing on *Survival of the Fittest* with the dedication usually only seen in marathon runners. Reading books, practicing fire building, studying native flora and fauna. She had the art of survival down pat. In a jungle, a woodland, even a cave, she'd be fine.

What she was not prepared for, however, was a lavish mansion with a manicured lawn and a butler waiting at the door.

She parked her Jeep out front and considered the address on the letter she'd received via Speedy Delivery Services that morning. Bowden, her regular delivery man, had waited for her to open the envelope because he knew how much she wanted this chance at the *Survival* contest. Once he'd seen the look on her face, he'd offered a congratulations, told her good luck and bid her goodbye.

But she didn't need good luck. She had skill, and during her twenty-six years Mattie had learned skill was what counted, not money, not connections, not beauty. On the field and in the game of life.

She glanced again at the opulent home, sitting like a gem in the early-July sunshine. It had to have at least twenty rooms, all behind a stone facade with great white columns flanking the front steps. This was the right street and number, but as far away from what Mattie considered roughing it as life could be.

Maybe she had to do publicity photos first or something. She'd seen CBS pull that on their contestants once. She wouldn't put it past the Lawford, Indiana, network to do the same.

She got out of the car, strode up the granite steps and raised the bronze knocker, lowering it twice against the matching plate. A moment later an older man wearing a black suit opened the massive eight-foot oak door.

"I'm here for the TV show," Mattie said, holding up the letter, her voice more question than declaration. This *so* didn't feel right.

The butler, tall, slim and gray, didn't blink. Or even seem to breathe. In fact, if she hadn't seen his hand twitch a little on the door frame, she'd suspect he was one of Madame Tussaud's best. "Right this way, ma'am." He stepped back and waved her into the house.

"This can't be right," Mattie said, entering the ornate marble foyer. A crystal chandelier hung over them, the cut glass reflecting like a constellation in the sudden burst of outdoor light. "I'm here for *Survival of the Fittest.* This looks more like *Day Camp for the Rich.*"

The butler merely walked down the hall without answering her. Mattie considered leaving. If this was the right place, though, and it was some kind of trick to throw her off guard before the real *Survival* contest started, then she might disqualify herself by walking away.

"So, do you have a lot of Girl Scout campouts here?" she asked as she hurried down the hall to catch up, looking around for hidden cameras.

"Excuse me, ma'am?"

"You know, sitting around the fire, singing "Kumbaya" and eating s'mores? Or is this more the place people go for serious mall withdrawal?"

"Uh, no, ma'am. We have none of that here at the James Estate," the butler said, without a hint of humor in his voice. He cast a glance over his shoulder at her flip-flops and khaki shorts, not bothering to hide his look of disdain for her attire. Apparently, guests who weren't properly clothed weren't allowed very far into the house because he stopped at the first room on the right, a fancy-dancy parlor well suited for a poodle, and led her inside.

"Please have a seat," the butler said, gesturing toward an ornate love seat with some curlicue fabric on it. She knew there was a name for the pattern—a name she'd never bothered to learn, much to the consternation of her mother, who thought living well was the only way to live.

Mattie, who'd spent her life with scraped knees and grass-stained socks, believed in playing hard and winning well. Curlicue fabrics didn't fit into that equation.

The butler cleared his throat. Mattie regarded the chair. It looked more like dollhouse furniture than people furniture. Still, the butler seemed convinced it would make a suitable seat.

"May I take your, ah, bag, ma'am?" He eyed her Lands' End backpack with a little confusion. She'd be willing to place odds on the number of people who came into a house like this ready for outdoor adventures.

"I'll keep it with me, thanks." On the other network's show, Mattie had seen what happened to people who made the mistake of giving up their stuff. They ended up stuck on some island with nothing while their smarter competitors remained fully equipped. That wasn't going to happen to her. She intended to win, and if that meant keeping her backpack away from the mortician over there, so be it.

She tucked it on the floor beside her feet and lowered herself to the love seat. No matter what it was called, the chair certainly didn't hold a lot of love for her rear end. The seat felt stiff and uncomfortable, as if it was layered with concrete beneath the fabric. She hoped she wouldn't be here long. Mattie Grant was about as well suited for an environment like this as a cheetah was for a cat carrier.

The butler backed out of the room, shutting the double doors without a sound. Mattie fished out the letter again from her back pocket. The single piece of stationery from the Lawford television station was simple and to the point, telling her she'd been selected as a contestant on their new reality show. The letter hadn't been very detailed, which she'd expected. When she'd gone to the tryouts for *Survival of the Fittest,* the producers had warned her they'd keep as much information secret as possible, but still…

This letter was taking subterfuge to a whole new level. It said little more than "Congratulations on being selected as a contestant on Lawford Channel Ten's newest reality show," the address to which she was supposed to report and the day, Tuesday. Nothing else specific at all, except the prize money amount.

Fifty thousand dollars.

"Fifty thousand dollars." Even aloud, the number sounded huge. She needed that money. She had to win. Even if it meant putting up with this environment for a while before she got to the place where she felt most at home—the great outdoors.

The doors opened again and in walked a man. Okay, not a man. A demigod. At least six feet tall, he had the dark good looks and deep-blue eyes that made grown women trip over themselves in order to get a better look. Sort of a Pierce Brosnan type, only younger.

Mattie figured she could take him. No problem.

A guy like that wouldn't last long in the woods. He'd be too worried about what gathering a few sticks of kindling would do to his manicure. Good. One competitor she didn't have to worry about.

"Am I in the right place?" He paused, adjusting his maroon tie.

What kind of guy wore a suit on a survival show? Well, there had been that lawyer on the other network's show two or three seasons ago. Maybe this guy had some crazy ideas about using his navy Brooks Brothers suit for a makeshift sleeping bag.

"Depends on where you're supposed to be," she said.

"Touché." He smiled. "I'm sorry. I probably should have started by introducing myself. I'm David Simpson." He took a step toward her, putting out a hand. "And you are?"

Mattie rose and shook with him, grinning. "Your worst nightmare."

"Excuse me?"

"Sorry. I'm Mattie Grant." She broadened her smile. "And I don't intend to lose this game."

He grinned. "And neither do I."

She gave his three-piece suit and polished shoes another glance. "I don't think you're quite cut out for this competition."

"Funny, I was going to say the same thing about you." He gave her the once-over, his gaze lingering on her shorts and flip-flops. "Aren't you a little…underdressed?"

"I'm not here for a beauty pageant. Who cares what I look like?"

He chuckled. "I like you, Mattie Grant. You aren't what I expected. This is going to be one interesting show," he said. "Very interesting."

He had a way of looking at her that was both direct and intent. Like he was sizing her up. Well, two could play that game. She circled the room in an idle pattern. "Why do you think they're doing a show like this in Lawford, of all places?" Mattie asked. "I'm not complaining, and Lawford is a good-size city, but this is usually the kind of thing the big networks do."

"Well, reality TV is low budget, big viewership. To the head honchos at Channel Ten, this was a no-brainer. The new station owner is hoping to make a big splash in this marketplace. Lawford Channel Ten isn't exactly the shining gem in the Media Star conglomerate."

Mattie cocked her head and studied him. "How do you know all this?" She didn't remember reading much more than a press release announcing the new station ownership in the *Lawford Sun*. Apparently David Simpson knew something she didn't know.

He had an edge. And Mattie didn't like that at all.

"I, ah, heard about it at work." David turned away and moved across the room to study a spring landscape hanging on the wall.

"Do you work in TV?" She tried to keep her tone casual, friendly. This not being a girly-girl thing made it tough, though. Even to her own ears she sounded like an FBI interrogator.

"No."

He didn't elaborate. She shouldn't fault him for that. They were, after all, competitors. Personal knowledge could be used to someone else's advantage. She wasn't about to share anything, either. No one here needed to know who Mattie Grant really was or why she was on this show.

However, that didn't mean Mattie couldn't find a way to soften her approach. How she'd do that, she had no idea. Her best interactions with men came when she battled them for a black-and-white ball on a hundred-yard field. This small talk in the parlor thing left her feeling like a cow trying to perform "Swan Lake".

Behind them another door opened and a woman in an evening gown—most likely Dior, said another part of Mattie that used to live a life where those kinds of names mattered—slipped into the room, her movements lithe and graceful. Her auburn hair was perfectly coiffed, her nails impeccably done, her presentation flawless.

What was with these people? Didn't they realize this was an *outdoor* adventure show? She'd never seen a survival show where everyone came dressed for the Oscars.

Either the producers for the Lawford television station had zero idea what a show like this comprised or…

For the first time that day, Mattie began to feel a little worried. *Had* she stumbled into the wrong place somehow? Had there been a mistake?

"Oh! I see you two have already met," the woman said, glancing at Mattie, then at David. "The butler was supposed to bring you to the dining room with the other men, but I suppose this one mistake won't mess things up too badly."

"Are you the owner of the house?" Mattie asked. Why wasn't she supposed to meet David? And what was up with this "other men" thing?

"Oh no! I'm Larissa Peterson, the host of the show." She put out her hand to Mattie and then to David. "The owners are in the Caribbean and graciously allowed us to use their home for the show." She looked around the room, empty except for the three of them. "I'd thought maybe someone had been in here already to explain everything to you."

"Wait a minute. You said you're the…host?" Mattie took another look at Larissa's designer dress and high heels. "Of *Survival of the Fittest*?"

"God, no!" Larissa laughed. "I couldn't survive five minutes outside of civilization. I'm the host of *Love and the Average Jill*."

"*Love and the Average Jill*? But…but—" Mattie's gaze zipped around the room again. The pieces fell into horrifying place, one at a time.

The letter that hadn't named any specific show.

The fancy mansion.

The butler who'd been surprised at her sporty attire. The man dressed in a suit. One of the...

Oh, God. Bachelors. *Plural.*

That meant she was supposed to be the...

"I think I'm in the wrong place," Mattie said, letting out a nervous little laugh. She choked back the nausea rising in her throat. No, no, *no.* This was *not* for her. She had to leave. *Now.*

Mattie pivoted away and yanked her backpack out from under the love seat. It caught on the bottom of the cushions before giving way, causing her to stumble a couple of feet.

David put a hand against her back, saving her from crashing to the floor. For a second she felt as if he'd zapped her with a stun gun. "Steady there. Don't want to hurt yourself before we've even begun."

She jerked away from his touch. This was wrong. *So* wrong. "I'm supposed to be on *Survival of the Fittest.*" Maybe if she said it enough, it would come true, but the sinking feeling in her chest told her something else.

Larissa laughed. "I don't think so. Do you have your letter?"

Mattie nodded. "Yeah." She dug in her back pocket, fished it out and handed it to Larissa. *Find the mistake, please,* Mattie prayed.

Larissa scanned the single sheet of paper, then looked at Mattie, considering her for a long, long moment. "You're Matilda Grant?"

"Yes, I am." Lord how she hated her given name.

Made her sound like a character from *Sabrina, the Teenage Witch,* not a woman trying to be taken seriously in a rough-and-tumble sport.

"You're not…" Larissa paused, put a finger on her chin, then her lips turned up into a smile that Mattie swore looked crafty. "Why, you're the *perfect* average Jill." Larissa put out her arms, as if she expected Mattie to step into the hug. "Welcome to the show, and to your heart's destiny."

At those words everything within Mattie rebelled. She put a hand to her stomach and dashed from the room before Lawford's newest bachelorette made an unforgettable impression on the Oriental rug.

Chapter Two

Mattie stood in the driveway, catching her breath. After a minute she got into her Jeep and turned the key. The engine made a sick "rew-rew" sound but didn't get any further than that.

"Come on, baby, not now," Mattie said. She turned the key again, whispering to the cantankerous ten-year-old vehicle. It didn't turn over. It just let out a high-pitched moan like a donkey refusing to make that last trek back up the Grand Canyon.

Clearly, a little Jeep revenge for missing that last tune-up and oil change, since money had been so tight lately. What she wouldn't do for a Jiffy Lube and a miracle.

"Damn!" Mattie smacked the steering wheel, but that didn't do anything more than hurt her palm. She dug in her backpack and found her cell phone. Within a few seconds she was connected with her best friend.

"Hey, Mattie. Are you surviving okay?" Hillary's voice traveled across the line, upbeat and positive as always. She could picture Hillary sitting at her desk at the Lawford Insurance Company, blond and fit, zipping through her day with the same enthusiasm she gave all her friends.

"Yes, but not on the show I thought." Mattie gave Hillary a quick rundown of what had happened. "Now they want me to stay and be on *Love and the Average Jill.*"

"I saw the previews on the news this morning. Looks like a great one." Hillary laughed. "And they asked you to do it? For real?"

"Yep. They've even got what I assume is a whole room of bachelors waiting for me, too. They said something about fifteen men. Fifteen! I don't think even Cleopatra had that many at once."

"Sounds like fun to me. A bachelorette party made in heaven." Hillary laughed. "So why aren't you in there?"

"Because that's the last thing I need right now. I'm not interested in falling in love or getting married, especially in front of a bunch of cameras. I'm here to raise money for the Lawford Girls' Soccer League. That's why I wanted to go on the Survival Show. I bet this one's "prize" is true love. I need cash for the league, not a man."

"I love your altruistic spirit, Mattie, but you should

think of yourself. How long has it been since you went out on a date?"

"What does that have to do with this?"

"Uh, excuse me? Did you not just tell me you're standing in front of a mansion filled with gorgeous men who want to date you?"

"Yeah, but—"

"But nothing, girlfriend. If you have any brains at all, which I know you do, you'll get back in there and get yourself one of the hot guys inside."

"Hillary—"

"Don't 'Hillary' me. You know I'm right. You've become a virtual hermit, pouring all your time into those girls' teams. Now, I know what you're going to say, so don't interrupt me. The girls need you and the league needs you. Everybody gets to have you but you." Hillary let out a sigh. They'd had this argument at least three times in the past six months, with Hillary always trying to get Mattie to go to a bar or a singles club or some other crazy thing that would take her focus away from her job and her girls.

She wasn't going to do that. Mattie Grant needed a man about as much as a monkey needed a second tail.

"Right. That's why this is a bad idea."

"No, that's why this is a *perfect* idea! It's going to be on TV, so you can get plenty of publicity for the league. And if you stick it out, the exposure can help you get the money you need to get it back up and running, plus keep you employed. What's not to like about it?"

"The dating part," Mattie said, toying with the steering wheel of the silent, recalcitrant Jeep. "That's not what I had in mind when I signed up for *Survival of the Fittest*. I was supposed to be out in the woods, trying to choose between poisonous and nonpoisonous wild berries, not standing in a mansion choosing a mate with all the forethought of picking a doughnut out of a box."

"I'm saying this as your best friend, Mattie. You need a man. A nice one, preferably. And now you have fifteen at your beck and call." Hillary laughed. "You are the envy of the entire female population of Lawford. So enjoy it while you can."

"I'd rather be out building fires and roasting wild game."

"If you're lucky, you'll get to do a little fire building still." Hillary laughed again, then said goodbye, with a second admonishment to Mattie to get back in there and get herself a man to go with that money.

Hillary was right about one thing. It had been a while since Mattie had been on date. That didn't make her a hermit, just—

Okay, maybe it did.

She took in a deep breath and looked again at the mansion. It was only a week. Surely she could last.

And besides, who said she had to fall in love, anyway?

David had watched Mattie Grant's mad dash from the room with sympathy. If he'd had a choice, he wouldn't be here, either, sacrificing himself on the reality TV altar, all to save his skin.

Actually, he'd had a choice, more or less. He could have kept his idea—which had seemed so sane at two in the morning when he'd concocted it after watching too many infomercials on how to get rich on hair removal products—to himself. But once he'd shared it with his editor, he'd been left with two choices: get the story or get another job.

Now he wasn't going to leave. He had too much at stake to back out.

"Well," Larissa said. "I'm sure she's just a little nervous. She'll be back." Though the hostess didn't sound as sure as her words.

David hoped Mattie would return. Having the star run out just before the show began would leave it a tad dead in the water. And would totally mess with his own plans to expose the reality show—and its competitors—for the crock of lies they really were. Happy endings and true love between strangers, matched up with an eye on ratings. Yeah, right. In the end, he'd expose the faux lovey-dovey characters as nothing more than people who were focused only on themselves…and the cash prize, of course.

Mattie Grant, however, wasn't at all what he'd expected. He'd thought he'd be stuck here for a week with some washed-up beauty queen with nothing on her mind but marriage. He hadn't been looking forward to that.

But Mattie…well she wasn't a beauty queen. Though

she had a killer smile, long blond hair and eyes the color of green gems. Okay, so she was a beauty. Just not a pageant kind of girl. She didn't even seem the high heels type. And that made her interesting, more so than he wanted to admit.

He'd felt a spark—hell, a jolt—when they'd shaken hands. It was something he'd have to ignore, because involving his heart or any other part of his body in this show was not in the plan.

He wasn't that kind of guy. He was good at staying uninvolved, uncommitted. In his twenty-eight years David had learned that even the people he thought could be trusted always kept something hidden, some nugget of truth they secreted away from others. It was far easier, he'd discovered, to pour himself into his work—the work of uncovering those lies—than to open himself up to others.

The door opened and Mattie came back in, a little paler than before. "My Jeep won't start. I need a few tools to clean off the plugs and wires to get it going again, but Stone Man doesn't seem to be anywhere around."

A woman who fixed her own car? David gave her a smile of appreciation.

"Stone Man?" Larissa asked.

"The butler." Mattie swung her backpack onto her shoulder. "You know, forget it. I'll walk. It's only seven or eight miles back to my apartment."

"No, wait. Don't go," Larissa said, stepping forward.

She seemed to be crafting a plan as she spoke. "You're already here. Plus, you signed the release when you sent in your application, so you agreed to participate then."

Mattie put up her hands. "Not on this show. I signed up for *Survival of the Fittest*. If you people don't have plans for building a lean-to in the rose garden, then I'm outta here."

"I don't think you're on the wrong show," Larissa said, coming up and taking her arm. David thought it looked more like a vise grip than a friendly touch. She withdrew a walkie-talkie from the evening bag at her arm and pushed a button. "Get in here. We have a...new twist."

"There's no twist," Mattie said, extricating herself from Larissa's grasp. "I'm not doing this show. I don't want to get fixed up or married. I want to prove my survival skills."

Larissa didn't give up easily. She draped an arm over Mattie's shoulders as if they were old friends and confidantes. "Mattie, isn't that what dating's all about? *Survival of the Fittest*?"

When Mattie opened her mouth to protest again, Larissa turned toward David. "Don't you agree?"

And then he knew for sure what Larissa was doing. Somehow, Mattie had been sent to the wrong address. Rather than try to find the real bachelorette, Larissa was working with what she had—a woman who seemed to truly fit the words *Average Jill*. Everything from Mattie's tennis shoes to her backpack fell into that category, and yet there was something about Mattie Grant. Maybe the way she held herself or the defiant spark in her eyes. Mattie was as far from average as a woman could get.

Mattie Grant also didn't seem the type to follow the rules.

He smiled. He couldn't have latched on to a better story if he'd tried.

"Well, David?" Larissa prompted, clearly trying to get him to take sides. "Don't you agree?"

Mattie scowled at him. David lobbed a grin her way, to show her that he had good intentions. She didn't return the volley. "I agree," David said to Larissa. "Dating is very much like a game sometimes. Sort of like doing crossword puzzles in ink."

"A man who likes a challenge, huh?" Mattie said.

"Always."

"With crosswords, you're only competing against yourself. Are you afraid of losing?"

"Never." David took a step closer to her. "Are you afraid of playing this game?"

Mattie's direct green gaze met his. "Not at all."

There was fire in her words—and a fire in his gut that hadn't been there five minutes ago. David cocked a grin at Mattie. A challenge indeed.

The doors burst open and a chubby guy in a beige golf shirt and khaki pants, wired up to a walkie-talkie ear piece and cell phone, headed into the room. He held a large order of fries in his free hand. Twin globs of ketchup dotted the front of his shirt like crimson buttons.

"What's up, Larissa?" He halted, took a long look around the room, then blinked twice at Mattie. "Hey, who's this? Where's Miss Indiana?"

"This is Steve Blackburn, one of the producers for *Average Jill*," Larissa explained. The she turned to Steve. "I don't know where Miss Indiana is, but this," she said, "is Mattie Grant."

"Who? What? This is going to totally mess—"

"When I saw her, I realized Mattie is the *perfect* Average Jill," Larissa went on, interrupting him. "A lot more perfect than a former beauty pageant winner."

"Oh, no, I'm not," Mattie said, backing away. "I told you, I'm supposed to be on *Survival of the Fittest*."

Steve withdrew a fry from the bag. "What do you do for a living?"

"I chair the Lawford Girls' Soccer League and coach two of the girls' teams. But I do *not* date fifteen—"

"Nice PR potential with that. Philanthropy angle and all that," Steve said, wagging the fry at her. Larissa murmured agreement. Then he turned to David. "So, you think she's pretty?"

"Definitely." Mattie had a natural beauty, unmarred by makeup or a frou-frou hairstyle. She had an unfettered, what-you-see-is-what-you-get-and-if-you-don't-like-it-tough look about her.

That interested him. On a purely reportorial level, of course.

"Good. Get over there and stand next to her." Steve

gestured between them, using the fry as a baton. "Go on, she won't bite. Will you?" He looked at Mattie.

"Of course not! What kind of person do you think I am?"

"I auditioned some of those girls trying out for *Survival*. They were a little, ah, hard core."

David crossed to Mattie, as he'd been told. He figured it wasn't a huge hardship to stand beside her and get a closer look at those bright green eyes. "Looks like we're a twosome."

"Not for long." Mattie scowled.

The producer and Larissa stood together, conferring. "We get a dress on her, she won't be so bad," Steve said.

Mattie put up her hands. "I'm on the wrong show. Aren't you people listening to me?"

The producer's phone jingled and he answered it, juggling food and electronics and managing to munch as he multitasked. "Yeah. So she's there now? How's that going?" He laughed. "That'll make good TV. Maybe serendipity had better plans than we did. Can you talk her into staying? Yeah we're set here. Things are working out," he eyed Mattie, "better than we expected."

Mattie turned to David. "Ever get the feeling they're seeing you as the goose who laid a ratings egg?"

"You going to stay?"

"Nope. This isn't for me." She swung her backpack over her shoulder.

She was going to bolt again. He needed to do some fast talking if he wanted her to stay, for the sake of his story.

"The prize money is the same, you know," he began. "*And* you don't have to eat bugs."

"There's prize money on this show?"

"Yep. Fifty thousand to the Average Jill just for suffering through all the dates and then a hundred-thousand-dollar purse for her to split if she falls in love and gets engaged at the end."

"Another fifty thousand if she falls in love?" Mattie's eyes grew wide. For a second David had to remember to breathe. It wasn't fair that one woman should have eyes that captivating. "With who?"

"With me, of course."

"You?"

He cleared his throat. Whoa. That hadn't come out as he'd intended. In fact, he hadn't even wanted it to come out. He wanted to last to the end of this game, to get the maximum bang out of his story, but he hadn't planned on broadcasting his strategy to everyone, least of all Mattie.

Besides, he wasn't here to fall in love. He wanted the story—not the girl. Work was what he'd always focused on, not relationships. Work was permanent, relationships were…not. "I meant with me or any of the other bachelors."

"Do I have to date *all* of them?" She pressed a hand to her stomach as if she were going to be ill.

"Do you have something against dating?"

"It's not something I do much of, as a rule."

They had that in common at least, though he didn't say it. "Why not?"

Mattie recovered her composure and parked a fist on her hip. "That's none of your business."

He grinned. "Well, it will be. Mine and, very soon, all of Lawford's." He gestured toward the doorway, where a cameraman stood, a camera over his arm. "Get ready for your moment in the sun, Miss Grant."

This was not what she wanted. She'd expected to be in the woods somewhere, in a state forest or on an undeveloped lake, fending for herself with a group of other competitors, using the skills she'd honed over years of Girl Scouts, camping and cross-country bike rides.

She had lived this fancy life a long time ago, until she'd left home, and then her mother's divorce had taken it all away for good. The mansion. The clothes. The silly focus on one's self.

She would have preferred to be in the middle of a forest with nothing but a pack of matches and a working brain to rely on. But there was the money to consider. Not to mention the good she could do with it. She didn't *have* to fall in love. She'd have fifty grand just for sticking it out.

It was survival, as Larissa had said. Just another kind. And besides, it appeared someone else had been sent to take her place on *Survival of the Fittest*, leaving her with one option.

Love and the Average Jill.

"Let's begin." Larissa moved to the center of the room, a wide, excited smile on her face.

"Already?" Mattie's voice came out like a squeak.

"Don't be nervous. You're perfect. The quintessential Average Jill. So much better than the former Miss Indiana." Larissa cupped a hand around her mouth and leaned toward Mattie's ear. "Who was about as average as a hibiscus."

Mattie wasn't exactly sure that was a compliment. After all, if the other woman was a hibiscus, what did that make her? A weed? "What do I have to do?"

"Enjoy yourself. The cameramen will follow you around all day but we only show an hour of the day's highlights each night and broadcast the elimination part live." Larissa gave her a wide smile. "Stick it out for a week. That's it."

"No strings?"

"No, none at all."

Mattie bit her lip. She glanced at David across the room, now talking to the producer. David hadn't seemed so bad. If he was the type of guy she had to deal with for the next seven days, she could make it through.

Heck, she could start a fire without a match and concoct a meal out of wild vegetables. How hard could this dating game be?

If she had known they'd be sticking her in a chair and putting makeup on her, she'd have backed out. Two hours later, Mattie found herself surrounded by the show's dream team—a hairdresser, makeup artist and clothing consultant, all assembled from the show's "headquarters" in the pool house behind the mansion to take her from average to…

Well, not average.

"Ouch! Don't do that," she said. "What are you doing?"

"Tweezing," the hairdresser, Pepper, said. He hovered over her with the torture implement, his bright-turquoise shirt and floral-pattern jeans a blinding combination. "Most men prefer a woman with two brows, you know."

"I'm not that bad."

Pepper took a step back, tweezers at the ready between his fingers, and analyzed her. "Not anymore, honey."

"Isn't this supposed to be about an *average* woman?" she said to Steve. He'd hovered in the corner the entire time, chomping on fast food and offering his input on everything from lipstick colors to heel height. "I'm not average if I'm all made up like this. Besides, this isn't even me."

And it hadn't been, not for a long time. At eighteen, when she'd walked away from the life of Chanel suits and Lancôme makeup, she'd vowed never to return. And now, here she was, starring in a bad sequel of her own past.

"This is TV. No one wants to see the real you."

"But—" Then she was cut off by Salt, the makeup artist and Pepper's partner in business, who had honed in on her with eyeliner. "Isn't this making me the exact opposite?"

Steve rolled his eyes. "Mattie, do you think anyone is going to tune in every night over the next week to see some soccer player get hooked up with Adonis? You may be cute in your cleats, but that's not what builds Neilsens."

She started to add to her argument, but Salt was coming at her with an eyelash curler, clamping it onto Mattie's eyelashes and warning her not to move.

She hadn't bought this many cosmetics in her lifetime, never mind worn them. And the clothes...

She cast a glance at the wardrobe hanging on the silver rod to her right. Some minion of Steve's had been sent scurrying to the Lawford Mall to come up with a bunch of suitable evening gowns when the producer had realized all Mattie had in her backpack was two pairs of denim shorts, a couple of T-shirts and a plain blue Speedo.

Apparently bachelors didn't go for women in Speedos. They wanted hot pink bikinis. Strappy gowns. Glittery tops and silky pants.

In other words, everything in Marshall Fields that made Mattie recoil in horror.

She endured Salt's eye makeover and told herself she could last through this. It was only a week. If she could stick it out until the end of this ridiculous dress-the-Barbie game, she'd get her money and she could finally take care of the people who needed her.

Then her mind went back to David Simpson. He seemed nice. Actually interested in her. As if he might want something more than simply winning the title of best bachelor and half the hundred grand.

Either way, if he, or any of the other guys, got any ideas about rounding any sexual bases, she had a way of taking care of *that*. When the men came on too strong—

She had a hell of a soccer kick to take them down.

Chapter Three

David Bennett stood in a semicircle on the back lawn of the mansion with the other fourteen bachelors and asked himself for the hundredth time why he was here. And more than that, why he stayed.

It was crazy to think he could come on this show and in a week pull his career out of the gutter. It had seemed like an awfully sane idea when he'd sent in the fake application. He'd put down a friend's name, not really thinking he'd get picked. His friend from college, David Simpson, was conveniently vacationing with his girlfriend and enough of a practical jokester himself that he found David's idea of borrowing the Simpson last name hilarious.

And then the letter telling him he was a contestant

had arrived and David had left his real name at home to find out the true story of these shows and blare it on the front page of the *Lawford Sun*. He had little worry about being recognized on camera. The one beauty of his job as a reporter was the visual anonymity. So he'd taken the monumental risk and gone on the show.

He needed to do something, especially after his by-line had been attached to that toilet of a story about the mayor's campaign contributions. His main source had turned out to be a pathological liar who thought he was the long-lost conjoined twin of Michael Jackson. That particular episode had been hard to live down at the paper. In fact, David was pretty damned sure they were still yukking it up at his expense over the Krispy Kremes in the break room.

So he'd taken on another man's name and filled out the application with enough dating buzzwords to convince the producers he was a lovelorn bachelor.

Albeit, after getting a look at Mattie earlier today, he would have to say this was one of the most attractive assignments he'd ever had. That in and of itself added a complication David hadn't counted on…but could handle.

With both hands tied behind his back.

"Hey, think she'll be hot?" One of the other bachelors, Kenny Wilson, said to David, elbowing him. "They always say they're throwing average girls on these shows, but come on, that doesn't make for good TV. Who wants to see an ugly girl fall in love?"

"Aren't we here to be matched with a girl for her personality, not her looks?" David said, repeating the show's tag line. He was acutely aware of the wireless microphone attached to his lapel, the battery pack clipped to his belt.

Kenny snorted. "Yeah, right. Since when did personality matter? I want someone so hot she's going to make me forget she even *has* a personality."

He couldn't stay here with a bunch of men like this— no, not men, Neanderthals—and last seven days. Plus, in order to make it to the end, he had to convince Mattie Grant he was the one for her.

It would be easier to convince his editor the Michael Jackson pseudo twin wasn't a complete fruitcake.

Larry Herman, another man who looked as if he was auditioning for *Cosmo*'s bachelor of the month, sidled up to them. "You're a hound, Kenny. Don't be drooling on her."

"I don't drool."

"You do, too. I saw you watching the beach volleyball competitions on MTV earlier and you were definitely drooling. I'm sure she's here looking for substance, not cream filling."

"Oh, and I suppose you have that?"

Larry puffed out his chest. "Sure I do. And a lot of it." He gave the other two men a wink.

"Gentlemen." Larissa, the hostess, glided onto the back patio in her second fancy dress of the day, her auburn hair back in a gold clip. She got their attention with a clap of her hands. "It's time."

"Man, I'm so nervous. I hope my deodorant works," said one of the guys on the far end.

"I'm sure she'll like all of you. This is your first meeting, so try not to be too nervous. This is a simple, getting-to-know-you cocktail hour. Mattie will be nervous, too, so be easy on her." Larissa gifted them with a smile.

"What are the odds *she's* free?" Kenny whispered in David's ear, motioning toward Larissa. "Maybe I could get a two-for-one here. Add in the fifty grand and I'm set for quite the par-tay."

"Don't forget you're miked, Kenny," David said. He bit back the urge to slug the insensitive clod.

"And now, without further ado, I'd like to introduce your lovely Average Jill, Mattie." Larissa took a step back, then waved her arm toward the wide French doors on the patio.

Mattie Grant stepped through them and onto the patio. She didn't glide in like Larissa had. She walked across the hard stone surface with care and a little bit of a wobble. In fact, the shoes didn't seem like they fit her feet or her personality. And yet, despite her obvious discomfort, she looked—

Transformed.

The staff had put her in a long green gown with black sparkles running along the sides, which accented her figure and redefined her hourglass. She had her hair curled and swept up into some kind of fancy style David knew the French had a word for. Soft gold tendrils curled around her ears, dancing at her chin. Red-painted toenails peeked out of strappy black heels, teasing from beneath the long gown.

They'd done her makeup. Her lips. Her eyes. She'd been gorgeous before, but now she was—

"Incredible," David let out on a breath.

"I've seen better," Kenny said. "But she ain't bad. Not exactly average. I told you so."

"She's stunning," Larry said, adjusting the mike on his collar. "You're just being a jerk, Kenny."

Mattie took several steps forward, each one less tentative than the last. When she reached the top of the stairs, she smiled at the group awaiting her below.

That's when David knew he was in trouble.

Mattie's smile, coupled with her eyes, held a power over him nothing else about her had. Together they had a way of drawing him in and holding him there, as if she were clasping his hand.

This wasn't going to be an ordinary story. He was fooling himself if he thought anything different. Reporter's distance be damned.

Her eyes scanned the fifteen men, finally settling on him, the one friendly face she knew. "Hi," she mouthed.

"Hi," he returned.

Kenny elbowed him. "Hey, don't horn in already. Give the rest of us a chance." He hustled past the topiary of green balls and around to the front of the group.

The three cameramen—their triangulated and choreographed approach as good as any SEAL team's—

started moving in, filming Mattie's progress as she made her way down the steps to the sloped lawn. On the third step, her heel caught in the stone and she tripped, teetering for a few seconds before gracefully regaining her balance and continuing on, as if nothing had ever happened.

"Think she's a klutz? Man, I can't stand a woman who bumps into things," Kenny said.

"And what are you, Mr. Perfect?" Larry said. "You don't have any faults?"

"Women love me. Faults and all." Kenny gave them his thousand-watt smile.

David could see why women might like a man like Kenny at first, assuming the man kept his mouth shut. He had cover model looks and probably acted charming in front of a female. But behind their backs, he became the Neanderthal he really was.

Mattie, David hoped, was smart enough to see through that.

Wait a minute, what was he doing? Thinking of her romantic future? He needed to plot a strategy for himself, not think about Mattie and whether she might fall in love with anyone here. It was a foregone conclusion. Mattie Grant was going to fall in love—or think she had—with him. She had to.

There was no other ending to this. It was the ending he'd already written in his mind for his story, the one his editor assured him would produce the biggest headlines. And thus save his career from being sucked down the sewer like a belly-up goldfish.

But as he watched her approach, her smile wide and open, he felt a twinge of conscience. A flicker of doubt. For a moment David wanted to chuck the whole thing and go back to writing obits.

Before he could envision the headline John Doe Leaves Two Grieving Dogs and Extensive Taxidermy Collection, Mattie was there. Her emerald eyes met his and his feet staged a mutiny against his best intentions, moving him toward her.

"Miss Grant, meet your bachelors," Larissa said, coming up beside Mattie and indicating the group with a wave of her arm. "They're a talented group of men ranging in age from twenty-two to thirty-one. We have a few entrepreneurs, a couple of MBAs and even an executive chef in our midst. Gentlemen, would you introduce yourselves to our Average Jill?"

They started at the far left. A lean, bespectacled guy in a navy suit stepped forward. His face reddened before he opened his mouth. "Pleased to…ah, pleased to…ah, well, I'm Bill." He blushed again and slipped back into line.

Mattie gifted him with a smile. "Nice to meet you, Bill."

The second guy, Rick, had more composure but offered up a lame opening line about hoping she'd be his destiny. David saw Mattie visibly pale at that. Tim gave her a smile and a sexy wink, implying more would be following from him than just his name. Then he blew his whole intro by telling her she looked even better than the fifty grand he could win. Gerry, the shortest of the bunch—and at five foot six, just about Mattie's height—didn't bother with an introduction, just coughed out his name and stepped back to his place.

There was some guy named Brock who flexed his right bicep as a way of showing off his best assets. Another named Rob who seemed all right enough, David supposed. Gave Mattie a compliment about her dress, shook her hand and then told her it was nice to meet her. Tom, who could have been blond Tim's twin, rushed forward with a hug that nearly bowled Mattie over.

Mark produced a flower—clearly stolen from the rose garden beside them—from behind his back and gave it to her, accepting full credit for his thoughtfulness. Three others whose names David didn't catch gave Mattie a salute and called her ma'am. Jim followed suit.

Larry ambled forward. "It's a pleasure to meet you. I'm Larry and I'm looking forward to getting to know you better."

"Thank you, Larry," Mattie said. David could see she was relieved Larry didn't try the half nelson that Tom did or the overblown intro of Rick.

Then it was Kenny's turn. He stepped forward, lifted Mattie's hand in his and raised it to his lips. "I'm eagerly anticipating the journey ahead," he said, his voice low. "My name is Kenny, but I don't expect you to remember it tonight. Later, I hope we have time to get to know each other. You, my dear lady, are already unforgettable." Then he lowered her hand and stepped back into place.

Just as David thought. Rico Suave on the outside, Cro-Magnon Man underneath.

The cameramen took a couple steps closer to capture the last introduction. David smiled at her as he moved forward and when she returned the gesture, something within his gut tightened.

How long had it been since a woman had made him react like that? With his instincts instead of his head? Already he was treading onto dangerous territory. Very dangerous. He could feel his objectivity slipping away, like water out of a sieve.

"I think you've made your impression already, Mr. Simpson," she said when he reached her.

Did she mean that in a good way? Or bad? He envisioned his head on the bachelor chopping block. "And so have you, Miss Grant," he replied. "As I said earlier, I expect this to be a very interesting adventure."

She grinned, cast a quick glance at the cameramen, then returned her gaze to him. "You have no idea how interesting it can get."

With that, David had no doubt he'd get his story. And maybe a lot more than he bargained for.

Mattie stood in a circle surrounded by a pack of men, feeling like the lone zebra at a hyena family reunion. She sipped from her champagne glass and made small talk.

And hated every second of it.

This wasn't her. This made-up woman with a crystal flute of bubbly and a Ralph Lauren dress. She'd feel more comfortable in a gorilla suit. In fact, she had been a gorilla once when she'd been the team mascot and donned the costume at games, running around the field and tossing bananas to the crowd. *That* had been fun. This was torture.

"Enjoying yourself?" Larissa asked, pulling Mattie to the side for a moment.

"Oh, yeah. About as much fun as doing my taxes."

"Oh, come on, all these gorgeous men are falling at your feet. It's heaven, not hell."

Mattie arched a brow. "This group needs something to do besides talk to me. Don't they want to go inside to watch the game or something?"

Larissa laughed. "They're here to fall in love with you, silly. Now get back in there and interact with them."

Fall in love with her? Over Mattie's dead body. She returned to the group, the cameramen dogging her every step, and was immediately taken into the one-upmanship huddle again. The men tossed out skills and hobbies like players at a poker game, each trying to up their ante in her eyes.

"This is nuts," she said to them. "I don't date like this, in a rotating pool."

The men all stopped talking at once. David caught her eye and sent her a grin. Of approval? Of mirth?

And what did she care, anyway?

"You guys want to get to know me? Then play *my* games." She hoisted up her dress to her knees, kicked off the abominable Feragamo shoes and then crossed to the topiary arrangements.

"You-you-you can't do that," Larissa sputtered. "What are you doing with your shoes? Your dress?"

"Being myself. I'm not some doll who makes small talk when you wind me up. Now get out of my way so I can have some fun." Mattie smiled. "Please."

Larissa's mouth opened. Closed. Opened again, then finally shut and she stepped aside. Mattie reached forward, jerked a topiary ball off the arrangement and tossed it onto the lawn.

"Now," she said, brushing her hands together, "who wants to be on my team?"

From across her makeshift field, David Simpson watched her with clear amusement. Something inside Mattie told her she was playing a game other than soccer tonight. For a woman who couldn't stand to lose, the odds were a bit too high for her liking.

The other fourteen men stood stone still in gaping surprise. Without thinking about the consequences, Mattie kicked the shrubbery soccer ball across the grass.

Straight into David Simpson's kneecap. He grinned, moved back and raised his wingtip into position.

The game had begun.

Chapter Four

Mattie had her foot poised, the ball in perfect position, about to score her fourth goal against David's team, when Steve came charging out of the house and across the lawn. "Cut!" he screamed, waving a half-eaten cheeseburger from a fast-food joint in one hand and a French fry in the other. "Cut! Cut! *Cut!*"

The cameramen jerked their cameras up and away from the action, then stood there, looking confused. David, who'd been guarding Mattie—and doing a terrible job of it because he watched her more than the ball—straightened and turned toward the commotion.

"Damn. I really need to stop saying Supersize me," Steve gasped, halting in front of Mattie. He bent over at the knees, breathing heavily, his belly heaving in and out with the effort. He took a second to catch his breath, then glanced up at her. "What the hell are you doing?"

"Scoring. Or I will when you get out of the way and let me hit the ball into the outdoor fireplace."

"This is not a soccer field. That," he pointed at the fireplace with the fry, "is not a goal." Steve sucked in another breath, then straightened. "And this is definitely not how a bachelorette should behave."

"Oh, yeah? Then how should I behave?"

"With decorum. Grace. Sweetness."

Mattie let out a curse that didn't have an ounce of decorum in it. "Then forget it. I'm not that kind of person."

"Why would you want her any other way?" David asked. "I thought this was a *reality* show."

"This," Steve indicated the topiary ball and hiked-up designer dress in Mattie's hands, "is a little more reality than I wanted."

"If you wanted a beauty pageant, you should have brought in a beauty queen," Mattie said. "I'm not about this life at all." She made a sweeping gesture that indicated the mansion and the fancy dress.

"Oh, but you are, Miss Grant," Steve said, his breath now fully recovered, and his gaze narrowing as he looked at her under the bright lights set up by the crew. "We checked you out, as we do all our contestants, and you're more suited for this than you claim." He took a step forward and kicked the ball away from her feet. "Now act the part you were brought here to play." Satisfied he'd made his point, he took a huge bite out of his burger.

"You…you—" she sputtered. How dare they do that? Delve into her past and then use it against her?

"Fifty thousand dollars," David whispered in her ear.

She cast David a glare that told him to butt out and let her handle her own arguments. "I don't want to win a dime if it means I have to be someone other than myself." She turned to Steve. "You asked for an average woman. You've got one. Now either be happy with me or find a new girl." She bent, retrieved her ball, and put it back where it had been. "Now if you don't mind, we only have five minutes left in our game. And I'd like to finish what I started."

Steve began to say something else, then bit it back as if he knew when he'd been beaten by a good argument—and a lack of a new Average Jill. He let out a frustrated gust, turned around and stomped back to the patio, waving his fry like a conductor, telling the cameramen to start again.

"You may have ruined things for yourself," David said, circling around to stand again between her and the goal. "They might kick you off the show."

"You can talk if you want, but you better play while you do it." She dribbled the green ball around him, judging where Brock might try to block her goal shot. He had his muscled arms up, but he hadn't squatted enough to block a header hammered straight between his feet.

David scooted around her again, causing her to rethink her position. And her level of attention to the game. With that piercing blue gaze of his that seemed to zero in on her with more precision than Beckham on a Puma ball, she had trouble staying focused on what she was supposed to do. If she could pay attention to the game—and not David—she'd be just fine.

On the makeshift field *and* this crazy reality show.

"Do you *want* to get off this show?" David asked.

"What I want is to keep my morals intact while I win the money." She dribbled to the left a few inches, raised her foot, then, just before she was set to hit the ball, turned it to the side and gave the ball a slight spin, which put it just past David's block and straight inside the fireplace. Brock had, as she'd expected, been too high in his defense.

David grinned. "You got another one by us."

"That's because you're too busy watching me to play." She ran after the ball, sent back to the halfway line by Brock for the next kickoff. Two minutes left of play and with most of the men already winded, she had a good shot at scoring again. The ones who'd opted for her team—Tom, Rick, Tim, Bill, Gerry and Mark hadn't had to do much more than block the opposition.

David jogged easily beside her, the one man who'd barely broken a sweat during the game. "I was *not* watching you."

"You might as well have suction cupped your eyes to my legs, for Pete's sake."

By the time Mattie got back to the ball, Kenny, the striker, had kicked the ball to Larry, who tried to pass it but was blocked by Tim, who sent the green shrub sailing down the field to Rick. Rick simply stood there on the field, looking a little unsure of what to do with the big green sphere between his ankles.

"You have nice legs," David said. "You can't blame a guy for looking."

"I'd rather men took *me* seriously than my body."

David slipped around in front of her, blocking her view of the game and disrupting her concentration once again. "What's wrong with doing both?"

She put her fists on her hips. "Oh, come on. You know men don't really do that. They're either body guys or mind guys. Never both."

"Body guys?"

"Guys who only want women for sex, not stimulating conversations."

"Well, I want more than just sex."

She snorted, jogged down the field and moved to the left, hunching down to anticipate Rick's kick, providing he could remember to pass the ball before Kenny or Larry stole it from him. The clock was ticking down, with less than a minute left. And still, Rick stood there, the ball securely tucked between his ankles, looking between the other men, trying to decide what to do. David appeared again at her side.

"You're telling me you came on a reality show to find a relationship?" she asked him.

"Yep."

"What's wrong with you?"

"Wrong with me?"

"Yeah. Why can't you meet a woman the old-fash-ioned way?"

"Oh, in a bar or at a second cousin's wedding?"

She laughed. "Yeah, like that."

"Because—"

Larry, who'd been designated timekeeper, stuck two fingers in his mouth and whistled twice, signaling the end of the game. Rick still held the topiary ball firmly between his ankles. If anything, he looked even more confused about what to do with it now that the game was over than he had before.

"Because why?" Mattie released the hem of her dress. It fluttered back to her ankles in a shimmer of sequins.

"Because I work too much to date. And my hours are bad for meeting people."

"Excuses," she said.

"Oh, yeah?" He fell into step beside her as they crossed the lawn and headed back toward the patio and a very-relieved-looking Steve, who was holding out Mattie's Feragamo shoes with a hopeful look. "Then what about you?"

"Me?"

"Yeah. Why aren't you dating?"

"Oh, I see. I ask you a question, you think it's fair to ask me, too." They reached the patio, and Mattie paused on the cool stone surface. "If I remember right, *I'm* the Average Jill. Which means I'm the one calling the shots and asking the questions."

Then she walked away from him, took her shoes

from Steve and slipped them on, a smile on her lips and a feeling that she'd won more than just a shrubbery soccer match.

"She wasn't what I expected," Kenny said a little while later, his breath coming in short, fast bursts. He, David and Larry stood to the side, watching Mattie talk with one of the other bachelors. In her hands she juggled the topiary ball—much battered now by their robust round of play.

David held a glass of wine one of the roving waiters had given him but he hadn't had a sip. All he saw was Mattie, her undivided attention on Tim as if he were the only man in the world.

A little flare of something stirred inside him. It couldn't be jealousy. He barely knew Mattie, and besides, he wasn't here to get involved with her, to care about her. He was here for a much more important purpose. Steve had mentioned something about her being familiar with living in a mansion. Seemed their Average Jill wasn't so average after all.

David had a hunch he'd just scored the first headline in his story. He swallowed back the twinge of conscience that pricked at him. She'd signed the permission slip for the show; she knew what she was getting into.

"Is she for you?" Kenny said.

"Huh?" David said.

"I meant, is she a surprise to you, too?"

"I guess. A little." Gee, with that kind of lying, his career in journalism was pretty much guaranteed.

"Well it should be fun to make her fall in love with me." Kenny grinned. "An easy task, of course."

"You think she'll go for a guy like you?" Larry laughed and reached for a Heineken in the ice-filled bucket of beers. The bartender popped the top, then offered to put it in a glass, but Larry waved him off. "You were breathing heavy before the first goal kick."

"Hey, I never claimed to be athletic. Just good-looking." Kenny grinned.

David swirled his wine, trying like hell to watch the Merlot slip up and down the inside of the glass, not Mattie smiling at something Tim had said. "A woman like her clearly wants a guy who has a little skill with sports."

Larry gave him a light punch in the arm. "Well, that isn't you. You missed scoring three times."

He had a damned good reason for that. Mattie had been right; he had been distracted. She'd hiked up her skirt, bent down to block his kick and her skirt had ridden up even further, revealing amazing legs. His concentration had flown to Alaska.

Larry took a long sip from his beer. "Those who snooze, lose the girl, you know."

"I'll be on my toes."

"Or on hers if you don't pay attention." Larry chuckled and headed in Mattie's direction. She turned to him when he reached her, gifting him with the same smile as she had Tim.

Clearly, she wasn't going to play favorites.

It shouldn't bother him either way. He wanted her for

the front-page headline her story would give him, not for a relationship. He'd been down that particular road before and had no intention of driving the love highway again. At least not without a much better seat belt and an airbag system.

David stepped back into the shadows and withdrew a tiny pad of paper from his breast pocket. He pulled out a pen and began making notes:

"The 'Average Jill' pretends to be interested in all the men. A tactic to avoid getting involved at all? Or a way to throw the men off track about her elimination round choices later? Or maybe she just likes the attention," he wrote.

Or maybe he was just too jaded by his job to see someone who was genuinely friendly.

Nah. David shook his head and glanced again at Mattie. She was heading toward him. David slipped the notebook and pen back into his pocket.

"Avoiding me?" she asked.

"No, not at all. Just grabbing some private time."

"None of it's private," she said, her voice low. "There's a camera on you right now."

The cameras. He'd forgotten them in the rush of the game and then his attempt to jot a few notes before he forgot them. He'd better be more careful next time. The last thing he wanted was his cover blown before he could get the scoop he wanted.

Perhaps…he could create his own scoop instead. Shake things up. Get Mattie Grant to lose her cool and give him something better to write about than how she made nice with everyone equally. "Maybe we should give the viewers at home a little water cooler tidbit."

"Water cooler tidbit?"

"You know, something they can gossip about at work tomorrow." He stepped forward, intending only to push her a little and see how she reacted to a male taking the lead.

But as he moved, he caught the scent of her perfume. If he'd been a novelist instead of a reporter, he might have described it as jasmine undertones with a bit of citrus, sexy and surprising all at once.

She swallowed, her gaze never leaving his. "I'm not the kind of girl who likes to be gossiped about."

He chuckled. "Then you picked the wrong show to be on."

"I didn't pick it, remember?"

"You think they wouldn't have gossiped about you on *Survival of the Fittest*?"

Her shoulders lifted and dropped in a shrug. "That would have been different. There I would have been in my element. But here—"

"Here you're not, Average Jill?" He stressed the last two words with an arch of his brow.

Instead of looking unnerved by his teasing, she seemed to draw up, as if steel had been injected into her veins. "I can handle myself with a bunch of men."

"As long as there's a soccer ball nearby, you mean."

"I don't need to play games to be in control."

"Pity." His gaze dropped to her lips, along with his thoughts. "I think games can be fun."

"And I think men with overblown sexuality are a pain in the butt." She cocked a smile at him, easing the blow of her words but leaving no doubt that she meant them.

"Are you speaking about anyone in particular?" He waved toward the rest of the men, grouped around the bucket of beers.

"If the shoe fits, Mr. Simpson, don't bother with trying another pair."

"Mattie's words of wisdom?"

She shook her head. "My grandfather's. He died last year," she added quietly. "Sometimes I think I miss his voice most of all."

Something in her gaze had softened, allowing a tiny bit of vulnerability to slip in. A sliver of remorse flickered in David, but he shook it off. The last thing he needed to do was to mix his job with emotion. Those two things went together about as well as bulls and the ballet.

And yet he wondered for a minute if she was real. The one unicorn he'd thought didn't exist in a world he'd come to see increasingly populated with con artists and thieves. David shook off the thought. He wasn't here to start believing in fairy tales or to fall in love with Mattie Grant. He was here to fool her into *thinking* he was in love with her.

None of the real thing allowed, not if he wanted to maintain any kind of journalistic integrity.

"I have to eliminate three bachelors tonight," Mattie said. "And before I do, I'll ask you the same question I've asked all the others."

"What's that?"

"Give me one good reason why I should let you stay instead of sending you home right now."

Chapter Five

Mattie watched David ponder his words before answering. A man who took his time before speaking? Or someone who was preparing before he sold her a darn good snow job?

She couldn't tell yet. Heck, she'd be lucky if she could ever tell. Dating games were not her forte. Put him on a field and she'd be able to anticipate his next move—as she'd proven tonight when she'd gotten the ball past him several times—but in the traditional one-on-one arena of boy-meets-girl, Mattie was usually caught without her shin guards.

"I don't think I'll give you a reason," David said after a moment. "You're a smart woman. I'm sure you can decide who goes and who stays without me pleading my case with a bunch of BS you don't need, or want, to hear."

She put a hand on her hip. Beneath her touch, the sequins on her dress rustled a little and pinched against her palm. "Or maybe you don't have a good answer."

"I don't need one." He gave her the same look he had given her when they'd first met, a mixture of teasing and maleness that had the damnable consequence of making her feel disconcerted. "I'm going to sell myself on personality alone."

"Glad to see there are still some bargains available in Lawford."

"Hey, that's low."

"I'm a midfielder. I can carry a low ball pretty far." Slipping into sports terms gave her a surer footing with a man like him.

He upped his home-field advantage by taking a step closer to her. The hum of connection simmered between them. "I guess that all depends on how well I can block you."

David Simpson didn't mean soccer. Her mental footing stumbled a little. "I've played goalie before, too. You can't outsmart me. Or outflank me."

"Maybe not." He considered her, one corner of his mouth turned up. "But I *can* outromance you."

By the way he was looking at her, liquid heat in his deep-blue eyes and a half smile on his lips, she had no doubt he meant what he said. She also knew, however, that David, like all of the other men, had come on this show expecting a beauty queen.

And finding instead Mattie Grant, average plain Jane.

"Why do you want to?" Mattie didn't kid herself about her desirability. There was a purse attached to her, one bulging with fifty grand. These men didn't expect to win her heart in a week. But they'd be crazy if they didn't hope to win a payday. "Why romance me? Is it the prize money? The competition?"

"If I tell you, I'll spoil my strategy." David's lips curved up the rest of the way. "I'm sure you know it's not smart to expose the game plan too early."

He'd surprised her with an answer that she had to respect. It wasn't the one she'd expected, nor was it like any of the ones she'd received from the other men. But it was one that spoke her language.

He was playing the game, just as she was. And for that, she couldn't fault him. In fact, she…well, she sort of liked him for being so honest about it.

Yet, something about David Simpson seemed to warn her not to get too close. A tingle of awareness that told her he was holding back, keeping parts of himself secret, as if there was a lie buried beneath a couple layers of truth in his words.

She shook off the feeling. They'd just met; it wasn't like she could expect them to become buddies over a glass of wine.

"You're not giving me much to work with here," she said, teasing him. "The other men all pleaded their cases."

He took another step closer, bringing his body so close to hers she could feel the heat between them, so much warmer than the July breeze circulating around them. "You need another reason to keep me here?"

"Or another reason to send you home." Her voice sounded shaky. She took in a breath, determined not to let him see he had unnerved her.

"I'm happy to oblige you, Miss Grant." Then David Simpson placed a finger under her chin, tipped it upward and met her lips with his own.

His kiss was nothing like what she expected. It was tender and sweet, yet sent a fire through her veins that told her she wasn't going to be happy with just tenderness. She closed her eyes, forgetting the cameras, the bachelors, the producer...

Everything she was supposed to remember.

His mouth drifted over hers, a caress. Desire surged within her, a feeling so foreign that she almost didn't recognize it. How long had it been since she'd allowed a man to get this close?

Too long, clearly. One didn't get this kind of satisfaction out of kicking a soccer ball, that was for sure.

Mattie raised herself up a little on her tiptoes, asking him to fill that gap in her body's résumé, to feed the want that seemed to multiply by the second.

But he didn't. David drew back slowly, his breath whispering across her lips. "You may send me home after that, but at least you'll send me home with something to remember."

Mattie opened her eyes and jerked herself back to reality—and reality TV. She'd just kissed her first bachelor in front of everyone in the mansion.

Not to mention the entire city of Lawford.

Well, her reputation as a serious soccer player was pretty well shot now. She might as well order pink tutus as the league uniforms and start a cabaret on the side.

"That…that shouldn't have happened," she said. "I had no intention of—"

"Kissing any of the men on a *dating* show?"

"Well, yeah."

He grinned. "I think that's an impossible goal."

She swiped a hand over her face, still heated from the awakened hormones rushing through her. Where was the soccer ball when she needed it to avoid this conversation and any more of this…

Oh, *this*. Her fingers lingered a moment on her lips, remembering. Memorizing.

"Maybe…maybe we should get something to eat," she said.

They walked together toward the buffet table. Behind them the trio of cameras trailed along, silent but watching. Always watching.

David cast a glance over his shoulder, then clearly decided to ignore the pressures of rolling video. "So, tell me about you, Mattie. Who are you and why are you on a reality show?"

Though she would have preferred to talk about the Pacers or the Colts, the change of subject from kissing was welcome. Anything that would distance her—and her mind—from his lips and everything still simmering inside her was a darn good idea, Mattie decided.

"Same reason most people humiliate themselves on television." She picked up a white china plate, then selected a few bites of cheese and crackers from the appetizer trays. Not her usual Ritz and Kraft. This was definitely the good stuff, the kind of food she hadn't eaten in years. "I'm here for the money."

His eyes widened with surprise and he paused in adding meat slices to a finger sandwich. "Most people don't admit the monetary motive, and if they do, they fluff it up with a bunch of bull about world peace and feeding hungry buffaloes or something."

"I'm not trying to win the money for me. It's for a dozen other girls."

He chuckled. "That sounds like a whole other reality show."

"It's not what you think." She popped a cheese cube into her mouth, munched it, then swallowed. "Like I mentioned when we met, I run the Lawford Soccer League. Or I used to, before it ran out of funding."

"I wro—" he cut himself off, started again "—read a story in the paper about that."

"If you saw it, you also saw it didn't exactly get front-page coverage. The reporter who did a story on us just wrote a few brief paragraphs and didn't even interview me or my team. Shoddy and lazy work if you ask me."

David coughed and speared a meatball with a toothpick. "Maybe he was busy."

"Yeah, well, that same reporter is always doing these exposé pieces three times the length of the itty-bitty piece on my league dying because of lack of funding. He has time to interview the mayor's mistress, but not me or my very disappointed team, which missed a whole season of play." She turned to the bartender, bypassed the wine and beer and instead asked for a diet soda on ice. "The power of the media, I've found, is often used for the wrong things," she said, pivoting back to him.

David gestured toward the cameras behind them, his now empty toothpick circling the air like a tiny wooden sword. "So your plan is to use the media by being on this show?"

She considered the trio of big black eyes that watched their every move. "Yeah, I guess it is."

"You surprise me, Mattie Grant. I didn't expect you to be so…contradictory."

"You make me sound like an unruly mule."

He laughed, a rich, hearty sound that escaped from his throat in a burst. She decided she liked the sound of his laughter and, for a second, imagined him laughing with her in a different setting. At a movie. A comedy bar. In her bedroom.

Whoa. What was she doing? Thinking about any of these men in a dating sense was crazy. It was exactly what the show wanted, and exactly what she *didn't* want. Mattie had one goal—to survive her time here without getting involved with anyone. She was here for her team, not for her own romantic future.

The little voice in her head reminded her she could win twice as much money if she fell in love. Fifty thousand, however, was more than enough for what she wanted to accomplish with the league. The full hundred thousand came with too many other price tags.

"I didn't mean you were mulish," David said, putting down his wineglass and withdrawing a Heineken from an icy beverage bucket, "just surprising. That's a good thing in a woman, in my book."

He grinned at her, and it seemed as if the heat of his gaze melted the ice in her drink. Best to change the subject away from her and onto him, before she went back to thinking about kissing him.

Whoops. Too late. Already did that.

"Speaking of books," Mattie said, "what were you writing in that notebook earlier?"

"You saw that." It was a declaration, not a question. She nodded.

"I, uh, write poetry."

"Poetry? You?" Of all the men standing on the mansion's lawn, David Simpson was the last one she would have picked to be composing haiku.

"Yeah. A little Shakespeare does a mind good."

"You…rhyme?"

"Well, not always, but I try."

She put her empty plate on the table and clutched the

cold glass of soda with both hands. "Well, David Simpson, you surprise me, too."

"Good." He grinned and tipped his beer toward her. "I hope that means I make it through the elimination round tonight."

"If you do," she said, not giving him any of her game plan, either, "you have to promise to read me one of your poems."

He swallowed. "Read you one of my poems?"

"I shared a bit of me. It's only fair you share a bit of you." She smiled at his clear discomfort with the request. Finally she'd found a way to turn the tables on David Simpson. "I mean, we are here to get to know each other, right?"

"Well, yes, but these are…well…personal."

"You were caught writing one on camera. The whole world knows now. Or at least the world of Lawford."

He opened his mouth, shut it. Then he took her hand in his and shook. "Sharing one of my poems it is then."

She'd won—sort of. As Mattie released David's grip, though, she had the distinct feeling she'd just made a deal with the devil.

Mattie stood in the ballroom of the mansion an hour later and faced the fifteen men who were there to win her heart—or Lawford Channel Ten's money.

Which was exactly why these men were wrong for her. She'd seen what happened when a relationship was based on a bank balance. There was no way she wanted that for her life.

The hardwood floor pressed against the Feragamo shoes, multiplying the discomfort of the high heels. Candles flickered from strategic places around the room, setting the stage for a show about romance. Pairs of red velvet chairs flanked little romantic table-for-two tableaus on either side of the room.

Anyone who walked in would think it was the perfect setting for a night of true love, but Mattie knew the truth. At the end of the room, the fifteen men stood in a semicircle, waiting for her to choose someone.

Mattie clasped her hands in front of her. The nearly overpowering smell of roses drifted from the vases set up on the mantel and throughout the room. Red, pink, white— it seemed like a valentine of bouquets. She hadn't seen that many flowers in one place since her grandfather's funeral.

Definitely not a good sign for what was supposed to happen in a few minutes.

Larissa came up beside her. "Ready?"

Mattie nodded. Her voice seemed to have fallen to her feet, pinched silent by the shoes.

Larissa put on a broad smile, then turned to face the camera on her right. "Tonight, Mattie has to eliminate three of the men who aren't right for her. She's had a chance to get to know all of them, albeit in a very…unconventional way."

From his position behind the cameramen, Steve

rolled his eyes. Clearly he still wasn't happy about her little impromptu soccer game. Maybe that had been a mistake. But heck, what did they expect? That she'd sit and have tea and crumpets with the men? That was not the kind of woman Mattie was. That was reserved for people like her stepsister Lillian.

Who was also working on husband number three, so clearly tea and crumpets weren't the way to meet a man. Or build a relationship.

"Are you ready to decide, Mattie?" Larissa asked.

She looked again at the men. Some had hope in their eyes; others seemed to wear an air of nonchalance.

It struck her that she'd be rejecting these men. Sending them home and rating them as somehow not good enough, when that really wasn't the case. She didn't want to choose—or not choose—anyone.

"Do I have to?"

"Well, yes, that's part of the show."

"But it seems so…mean."

Larissa smiled. "They're expecting this, you know."

She glanced again at the men. Many of them she'd only had minutes to get to know. How could she make this kind of decision? Nobody showed their true colors in that short a time. Heck, she was only dealing with black-and-white versions right now, not the true selves of these men. "I think I need to get to know them better first."

Larissa cleared her throat. "Uh, Mattie, this part's live and we only have sixty seconds until we go to a commercial so you better figure out who stays and who goes."

"Sixty seconds?"

"And counting." Larissa gestured toward the men. "And the first bachelor to go home is…?"

Tension twisted in Mattie's gut. Her gaze traveled down the line, starting with David and ending with Rick. None of them stuck out as Ogre of the Year. None screamed to be released from this farce of a dating game. Who would she choose? Jeez. It wasn't like picking out melons at the market.

"Uh…Tom," Mattie said, and immediately wished she could take the word back. She'd played on sports teams—and she'd grown up a misfit in her mother's fancy house—she knew what rejection felt like. The last thing she wanted was to do that to someone else.

But she had to do it. She couldn't get the money if she didn't. So she called up Tom, and only because he'd hugged her like an overeager politician. That full-body tackle had been a little scary. If she had to choose anyone, the mad grabber seemed the most logical choice.

Tom had moved forward and stood in front of her, waiting for her to say something.

"I'm sorry. It was very nice to meet you, but—"

Her words were cut off by a second, even stronger hug. "That's okay, I understand." He squeezed her until her breath squeaked out, then let her go. "Thanks for the opportunity." He turned to Larissa, dispensed a quick, tight hug to her, too, then walked away. Mattie could swear she heard Tom sniffle as he left.

One down, two to go. She glanced at David Simpson, swallowed back her regrets and called the next name.

Lawford Channel Ten was exploiting both shows for every minute they could get. Each night they condensed the entire day's worth of shooting into an hour-long show and ran any extra-juicy footage as a teaser during commercial breaks of other Channel Ten shows. Bowden Hartman had watched both *Love and the Average Jill* and *Survival of the Fittest* last night, but was treated to highlights when he walked into work and saw the morning news on the TV in the break room.

"Check it out," Jimmy said as Bowden poured himself a cup of coffee. "They're showing Miss Indiana trying to start a fire again."

Bowden glanced at the TV and saw the beauty queen, bent over a pile of wood, a curse word bleeped out every three seconds from her steady stream of complaints as she attempted to ignite a spark by rubbing two sticks together. Her high-heeled sandals kept her at a precarious perch over the kindling.

She had on a red satiny skirt that had become dirty over the course of her day in the woods and now sported a ripped seam up the left side, giving Lawford an extra viewing area. Her sequined blouse seemed to be missing a little of its sparkle. Bowden suspected it was decorating the dense foliage of the survival setting. Around her, most of the other eleven contestants watched her futile attempts with clear amusement.

Not one offered a hand—until Miss Indiana flashed that winning smile at one of the men and shrugged helplessly. He nearly sprained an ankle trying to scramble over to help her.

Clearly she'd learned to use *other* fire-building skills to help her survive in the woods.

The newscaster switched to the *Average Jill* update. Bowden smiled. There was Mattie, on the pedicured lawn of the mansion, kicking a—was that a piece of shrubbery?—around with the men in a rousing, competitive soccer game. She wasn't what the producers expected, he was sure. And that was what made it so much fun.

"Ratings for last night's airing of *Average Jill* far surpassed producers' expectations," the slim brunette newscaster said. "Steve Blackburn, the show's producer, said Mattie Grant's appearance on this show—instead of Miss Indiana, who was rumored to be the scheduled bachelorette—was a planned move."

"We wanted a real Average Jill," Steve said into the camera. "And we've got that and more in Mattie Grant."

Bowden grinned and sipped at his coffee. The producers were happy with the "slip." His job was secure.

Time to ratchet things up a little more.

Chapter Six

David erased the Microsoft Word file on his laptop for the fourth time that morning. He'd gotten up at the crack of dawn and Googled Mattie Grant.

And found what he was looking for.

For the first time in his career, though, unearthing a piece of information didn't send the familiar rush of adrenaline pumping through his veins. He stared at the information on his screen:

Stephen Kincaid, owner of Kincaid Wire Company…Kincaid, ousted from the board of his own company early last year for squandering corporate dollars on personal perks…divorced four times in acrimonious splits due to contested prenuptial agreements…father to one child, Jillian Kincaid, his child with second wife Delia, and Matilda Grant. Matilda is the daughter of Delia and sports agent Edward Grant…Edward died when Matilda was three…Delia married Kincaid one year later.

Kincaid was exactly the kind of man David usually went after. He was corrupt. Bad to his wives. Probably had a few dozen skeletons stored in his closet.

Was Mattie one of them? Did she have a few of her stepfather's bad habits? Or was she as sweet and nice as she portrayed herself?

Either way, she was the stepdaughter of one of the richest men in the city. That made her much more than your ordinary switched bachelorette. That made her not just a *story,* but a big, career-changing story.

But every time David put his fingers to the keys, the image of Mattie's smile came to mind. He knew she slept on the floor below, separated from the pack of men by the steady watch of the butler she'd dubbed Stone Man. Their ranks had been reduced last night when she'd sent home Tom, Tim and Rob, leaving twelve bachelors. Three more men were going to be eliminated tonight, Larissa had said just before sending them all off to their rooms last night.

With the subject of his exposé so close at hand, he felt…regret. It wasn't a normal feeling, certainly not one that came about often in his job. He'd learned long ago to tamp down his emotions because all they did was interfere in getting at the truth.

And if there was a lesson David had learned, it was that everyone lied at one time or another. Even women with beautiful eyes. His last girlfriend had been like that. Pretty, but only out for number one. He needed to keep that in mind.

His cell phone vibrated against his hip and he flipped it open, extending the antenna and crossing to the window on the far side of the den. He'd locked the door behind him when he'd snuck in here earlier, but just in case, he kept his voice down. Those cameramen never seemed to rest.

"Hey, Bennett, what do you have for me?" Carl Klein, his editor, barked over the line. David could picture him at his desk, already on his third cup of coffee and fourth cigarette, at a time of day when most people would still be sleeping. Carl was an insomniac who preferred to get to work early and label anyone who came in after him lazy.

"Uh, not much yet."

"Come on, that's not like you. You can ferret a story out of a dead raccoon on the highway."

David had something, but he wasn't ready to share it yet. He would eventually. He had to, considering his job was on the line.

"So tell me about this Mattie Grant," Carl said. "Do we have anything on her?"

"She's not that kind of woman, Carl," David stalled.

His editor snorted. "Everyone's that kind of person, Bennett. Dig deep enough and you'll find something."

The line hummed between them. Carl was waiting

for David to toss him a nugget of gossip to show he was doing his job. His editor had made it clear last week that David was replaceable, and this story was his last chance at redeeming himself as a valuable member of the paper's team.

David leaned his head against the hard oak window frame. The sun was just edging its way into the sky, casting purple light over the perfectly laid-out gardens. "Remember that soccer league I did a story on a couple months back?"

"Soccer league?" Carl said. On the other end, David could hear him take a sip of his coffee while he thought. "Uh, was that the one run by the stripper?"

"No. That was the senior men's baseball team. This was a league for girls. Designed to help disadvantaged teen girls get soccer scholarships." That had also come up in the Google search. Once again, David felt a pang of remorse for not doing his homework when Mattie's league had first been going under. Could he have headed that off by giving her more than three paragraphs on the obituary page?

"It's not hitting anything on my radar screen." Carl laughed. "Then again, it's not exactly the kind of story that would. Sounds like one of those feel-good Friday pieces I despise. Good news and all that. Who wants to read about good news?"

David almost said he did, then caught himself. He needed some coffee. His brain was turning to mush and making him sentimental. "Well, Mattie runs that league."

"Did she abscond with the funds or anything?"

"No, I don't think so." Though he made a mental note to check into that. Kincaid had done it with his company. Was his stepdaughter capable of the same thing?

"Well, find something out. An average girl living an average life doesn't sell papers, Simpson." Then Carl clicked off.

David turned off his cell phone. For the first time since he'd seen the word *journalist* on his business cards, he hated himself for what he was about to do.

"This is what you'll be wearing for your date today," Larissa said, handing Mattie something that looked more like embroidery floss than clothing. "Today's outing is the first of several group dates you'll be going on, to give all the men a chance to get to know you. And vice versa."

"Uh…what is that?"

"A bikini." Larissa smiled. "I think it's going to be wonderful with your coloring." To prove her point, she held up the hot-pink two-piece and pressed it against Mattie's chest.

"I have a Speedo. A one-piece. *Also* perfect for my coloring."

"Oh, I'm so sorry," Larissa said, not looking a bit contrite. "There was a laundry accident with your Speedo. A dryer run amok."

"You ruined it on purpose so I'd have to wear this thing."

Larissa smiled again. "Not me."

Mattie would bet a million dollars someone had intentionally ruined her conservative swimsuit, leaving her with no choice but to wear this one. "Well, wherever I'm going, I'm sure shorts and a T-shirt will work."

Larissa shook her head and dangled the swimsuit in front of Mattie. "Not at the WaterFun Water Park."

"I'm going to a water park?"

"You and three of the men. It'll be fun."

Mattie looked again at the fuchsia swimsuit. Fun? To walk around in public with three men, while the cameramen captured every thigh jiggle?

She'd rather be strung upside down over a pit of Madagascar cockroaches.

Well, maybe not. Bugs weren't exactly her favorite thing.

"Do I have to do this?"

"You're ours," Larissa said, that smile still on her lips. "According to the agreement you signed."

Mattie thought of her team. Only six more days to go, then she'd have the money, and her league could be started again. Those girls needed the soccer league, not just to learn the sport, but because it gave them an inner strength and confidence in themselves that Mattie knew from experience wasn't easy to find.

For them, she'd wear this silly suit.

Sort of. If there was anything Mattie was good at, it was developing a back-up plan.

"I'll do it," Mattie said, taking the suit and trying not to blanch at how light and airy it felt in her hands.

"Wonderful. The men are going to love this date with you."

Mattie grimaced. "That's what I'm afraid of."

When Steve came into the dining room after breakfast on Thursday morning and told Larry, Bill and Rick to put on their bathing suits and join Mattie for a group date at the water park, David had the strangest urge to commit bachelorcide.

He told himself it was because he was missing out on his story, that being left behind—from a bikini date no less—didn't bother him on a hormonal level at all.

Yeah, right.

The only thing he'd thought about since yesterday had been kissing Mattie and the feel of her in his arms. The way she'd kissed him back—so gently, yet with a buried passion that told him she was more than he'd bargained for—made him wonder once again if she and this show weren't the wrong subjects for his story.

She didn't seem average at all; at least, not what constituted average in David's world.

"Uh, I don't think so," Rick was saying to Steve. His face had paled and he had a hand over his stomach. "I, uh, had too much shrimp last night and well, I don't feel so good."

"Buck up, buddy. Mattie's going to be in a bikini. Doesn't that make you feel better?" Steve winked, then dug into a bag of French fries. Quite the breakfast, David thought.

"No." Rick sent a sickened glance at the fast food, then gripped his stomach tighter and groaned. "I gotta go."

"On the date?" Steve asked.

"No. *Definitely* not there." Rick turned and dashed from the room.

"Seems the shrimp wasn't so fresh," Larry muttered. "We've got two other guys down in the back bedroom."

Steve reached into a small cardboard box. "I'll have to draw another name for the group date since Rick is, ah, indisposed." He pulled out a piece of paper, righted it, and read the name on it. "David. You up to this?"

"Absolutely." David had never been so grateful for his dislike of seafood before in his life.

Because it would allow him to get closer to his story subject, of course, and not because it meant he was going to be seeing Mattie in a lot less than an evening gown.

He'd met some pretty convincing liars over the course of his career. When he slipped into the bathroom to change, though, he had a feeling the biggest liar was the one looking back at him from the mirror.

When Mattie arrived at the WaterFun Water Park and saw the three men standing at the entrance waiting for her to emerge from the limo, she considered faking a broken hip. Or typhoid fever. Anything to avoid getting out of the car in little more than a bra and panties in front of Lawford Channel Ten and a trio of eager, smiling men.

Larissa had told her she needed to go on three rides with the men, giving each man equal time alone with her. Well, all the cameramen would see would be a pink blur because she intended to get through this torture as fast as possible, dive back into the limo and hurry to the mansion for clothes that didn't make her feel like one of Hugh Hefner's girls.

Among the trio waiting for her, she saw David. The memory of his kiss hit her in the chest, knocking the wind out of her like a hard block from the opposing team. No. She wouldn't go there. Not today. Or tomorrow. She was going through all this TV stuff for her league, not herself, and she only needed David right now as an ally. Nothing more.

Time to put her contingency plan into action.

Mattie sucked in a breath, screwed up some bikini-wearing courage and stepped from the car, the two-inch heels of her matching sandals clicking against the pavement. The three cameramen piled out of a white van behind her, clocking her every movement, listening to every peep she made on the waterproof mike attached to her suit.

When they saw her, the bachelors seemed to stop breathing. Their eyes widened, their jaws went slack.

So this was what feminine power was like.

Once she'd escaped her mother's control at eighteen, Mattie had stopped dressing up, wearing makeup and doing anything fancy with her hair. For too long, people had seen her as the stepdaughter of Stephen Kincaid, and expected her to look, act and even walk a certain way. But two years later, when Kincaid had left her mother—and left her pretty near penniless in a crafty divorce that unearthed a prenup her mother hadn't realized had been so restrictive—so had those societal expectations.

Mattie had shed them all with gratitude, sure that being seen in her natural state was the only way to be seen.

Now, however, with three men practically incapacitated just watching her walk across a parking lot, she wasn't so sure the natural state was the only choice. Certainly, this was easier than kicking a soccer ball into their shins. And nicer to their tibias, too.

"Hello, gentlemen," she said. Jeez. Had her voice dropped into a lower range, too?

The men nodded, mute as bunnies.

"I'm looking forward to spending time with each of you today." She added a smile.

That worked even better. The bachelors moved forward, widgets on an assembly line.

She hated to admit it, but she liked this. Mattie cocked her head a little to the right, as she'd seen Larissa do once. All three men stared at her with goofy, happy smiles.

Hmm… This was going to be—

Then, out of the corner of her eye, she saw her worst nightmare approaching. Six of the girls from her league, clad in swimsuits, wet hair hanging down their backs, clearly here for the day. They were laughing and chatting as they made their way along the asphalt path of the water park from one ride to the next.

Oh, no.

Mattie straightened and wiped the flirt off her face. "David. I need a favor."

"Anything." At least he had recovered his voice box, though his gaze hadn't yet made it above her neckline.

"Give me your T-shirt."

"My…T-shirt?"

"Please." She put out her hand. *Do it fast,* she thought, *before anyone comes along and sees me.*

The girls from her team had stopped at one of the snack booths and were discussing the list of offerings. They hadn't noticed Mattie yet, thank God.

"May I ask why?" David said, his hands on the hem.

"Because I'm a little, ah, *naked* here."

"And what's wrong with that?" He grinned.

She gave him a glare. "I said please."

"When you ask so nicely, how can I refuse?" .

When David lifted his arms and removed his T-shirt, Mattie wondered if this was such a good idea after all. David was clearly a man who spent time in a gym. Okay, a lot of time. His chest was hard, his abdomen ripped, with the six-pack ridges that most men envied from their sofa cushions.

"Here," he said, handing it to her. She slipped it over her head and it settled against her skin with ease. The material was warm and carried the scent of him, a slight blend of musk and nature.

"It's too big," he said. She could hear his disappointment at the roomy shirt.

It wasn't too big, it was perfect. She was now covered from neck to thighs with a white-and-red Indiana University T-shirt that gave only a hint of the hot-pink nothing that lurked underneath. She still didn't want to run into her team, but at least she'd feel more like herself and less like a *Playboy* model if she did.

"Well, shall we get started?" she asked the men, gesturing toward the first set of rides. People careened along the plumes of water, shrieking their way down.

"You sure you want to wear that T-shirt?" Larry asked. "I mean, it might get wet."

Mattie grinned. "I'll be just fine."

"Yeah, I'm sure you will." Larry's mouth turned down, his plan at restoring her bikininess foiled. The three men walked along beside her, clearly missing the pink two-piece.

Good. Maybe they'd stop looking at her through the eyes of bachelors and instead see her as an equal. Well, maybe not just an equal—but also a woman who could kick their butts on a soccer field.

They approached the Tower of Chance, a twenty-foot pinnacle with a gushing waterfall that shot into a series of slides and spirals before ending in a deep, tranquil pool. A teetering stack of blue inflated rafts-for-two waited at the bottom for the riders to take up the stairs and use for their ride down.

"Who's first?" Mattie asked. "Bill?"

"Uh, that's pretty high," he said, pushing his tortoise-shell glasses further up his nose. "Are you sure you're up to that, Mattie?"

"That? It's nothing. I've ridden worse at Cedar Point."

"Didn't you hear that kid screaming on the way down?" He sounded terrified. Are you sure this ride is safe? I mean, the statistical probabilities of a fall—"

Mattie put a hand on her hip. "You're not scared, are you, Bill?"

"Of course not." He drew his shoulders back and directed his chin toward the rides further down the path. "I think the Lazy River's a little nicer for some alone time. We could ride and talk about your investment plans for your half of the prize money."

The Lazy River was *not* in her plans for today. That was too cozy, too intimate. Too much time to do nothing but float and talk—and get close to one of the bachelors. Nope, not on the agenda. Her plan was to get in the park, get through the rides and get out of this swimsuit as soon as possible.

"Is that Miss Grant?" Behind her, she heard the voice of one of the girls on her team.

She needed time to formulate an excuse, something that would allow her to work in her usual advice about female empowerment and choice, yet justify the bikini wearing and the cameramen.

"Let's go," she said, grabbing Bill's hand.

"Now?" he squeaked. "On *that?*"

Mattie bit back a curse and released the reluctant bachelor. She didn't have time to wait for Bill to gather his courage. "You can go on the next one then."

"I don't know, maybe," the girls were saying behind her. "It *kind of* looks like her from the back."

Mattie turned to the next man in line. He had a slight smirk on his face as if he was more than ready for the Tower of Chance and anything else she might offer. "David? What about you?"

"I'm game if you are."

"Good." She grabbed his hand with one of hers—lest he try to back out and delay her any further—then jerked a raft out of the pile and headed up the wooden stairs two at a time.

"That can't be Miss Grant," Corrine's distinctive throaty voice said. "She's holding hands with a guy and wearing makeup."

Mattie would have never thought her best disguise would be Cover Girl.

As for the holding-hands-with-a-guy part, the girls were right—she wasn't the type to be holding hands with a man in public.

Or enjoying it this much.

She refused to dwell on how David's palm fit perfectly into hers, how his larger fingers closed over hers with a feeling that bordered on security and comfort. How, for just five seconds, she'd wondered what it would be like to trust him, to cave in to the hot surge that had rushed through her when she'd touched him.

"We better hurry," she said, pushing those thoughts away. "That line is filling up pretty fast."

"When people want something, they go after it." David gave her a grin.

She let go of his hand and whatever meaning was hidden in those words and started up the winding wooden steps that led to the top of the tower. As they inched their way behind the other riders, Mattie started to notice how very high it was. From the ground, it hadn't looked like such a long climb. But once she reached the upper levels and looked down, it seemed like the highest water ride she'd ever been on. Maybe Bill had had the right idea. The Lazy River seemed like a darn good choice from here.

In fact, it looked like a darn good choice for the ant-size humans she saw circling around it.

"Scared?" David asked.

"Not at all." She grinned.

"If you get nervous, you can always hold on to—"

"You, right?"

"I was going to say the raft. It has these handles on the side." He pointed to one of the sturdy rubber grips on either side of the two-man raft. His smile told her he knew the tease had had its effect.

Men. This was exactly why she didn't need one, because they played games she had no hope of gaining an advantage at. "Good thing there are four handles. Two for me and two for you."

"If I get scared," he said, leaning forward to whisper in her ear, "I'll just hold on to you."

Something deep inside her, awakened by his kiss that first night, roared to life. It wasn't fear of the ride. Or of the consequences of having her life be on camera for a week. It was something new and foreign.

And scarier than all of that put together.

She cleared her throat. "You should be careful I don't suddenly twitch and toss you off the raft."

"You wouldn't."

"I would," she said, turning to catch his deep-blue gaze before moving up to the next step, "and I will."

"How do you expect to fall in love if you throw the bachelors off the ride?"

She pivoted toward him on the landing at the top of the stairs. "I'm not going to fall in love."

"But isn't that in the rules of the show? Or at least the audience expectations?"

"All I have to do is make it to the end, and I get fifty thousand dollars. I told you I don't need the full hundred thousand."

"But what if this is your one chance to meet the man of your dreams?"

She rolled her eyes. "On a reality show? I don't think so."

"Stranger things have happened."

"Yeah." She poked a finger at his chest, and couldn't help but notice how tanned his skin was. Whatever was stirring inside her seemed to take on a life of its own. *Kiss him again,* her mind whispered. She shushed it and reminded herself the bachelors were a means to an end, no matter how well one of them kissed or how much she had enjoyed it. "Maybe *you'll* end up falling in love."

The air between them seemed to quiet, as if for that split second everyone on the ride had stopped screaming, the water had stopped rushing past them, the wind had stopped whistling in the trees.

"I'm game if you are," David said.

"Game?" The word came out in a breath.

Kiss him, her mind whispered. *Now. Before—*

He gestured ahead of them, at the waiting staffers on either side of the giant slide. "It's our turn."

"Oh. Oh, yeah." Mattie shook off David's comment. He'd been talking about the *ride.* Not her and him. Thinking otherwise would lead her down a path she had no intention of taking.

Mattie slipped into the front position on the raft, if only to avoid him and everything she'd thought she'd read in his gaze. From there the drop down looked very, very high. And scary. "I think I'd rather sit in the back," she said, switching to the opposite position. "That way I can hear *you* screaming."

He gave her a smirk, then seated himself in the front. She'd forgotten, with him in the front, that her legs had to slip onto either side of his hips. The slippery contact had her mind going down the path she'd been trying to avoid all day. As much as she could, Mattie drew herself back and to the side, but still, her thighs touched his and she knew there was more between them than just a raft.

Each of them grasped their handles. Mattie's stomach plummeted and her heart seemed to scurry away to a hiding place inside her body as the staffers counted down and readied their push.

"One…two…three!"

Then they were off, zooming down the jet stream of water at lightning speed, careening around the curves of the plastic slide, looping up so high it felt like they would surely tip over, then slipping down and up the other side in a wild, topsy-turvy race to the bottom.

"Yeehaw!" David shouted.

Mattie let out something just as loud but a little less ladylike. The water sprayed her body, her hair, her face, splashing into the raft and over them. They circled a spiral as quickly as bubbles going down a drain, then zoomed up a small hill and down the last long, fast drop.

Unable to maintain her precarious position any longer, Mattie let her legs press against his. Heat zipped up her skin, made even more intense by the water and the speed beneath them.

The raft pitched forward, thrusting her against David's back. Without thinking, she let go of one of the raft's handles and wrapped an arm around his waist, pressing her head against his bare back, to block the spray and feel the contact of something solid. That feeling of security and comfort returned, and for the first time since the raft had left the top, she felt…

Safe.

Her stomach had deserted her, and a dizzying feel-

ing of fear and exhilaration filled the space in her abdomen. There was something else there, too, something
Mattie refused to name. Refused to acknowledge, because doing so would open up her heart to feeling.

She wasn't going to do that. He was here for the
same reason as all the others—the money. And she was
kidding herself if she thought differently.

Finally the raft curved to the right and slid into a deep
pool of water, drenching them both. Once she went
under, Mattie released David and pushed herself up to
the surface.

"That was fun!" She pushed her hair off her face,
laughing. "And terrifying."

"I couldn't agree more." He grabbed the floating raft,
and together they made their way over to the edge of the
pool before the next set of riders came plunging into it.
"You weren't, ah, holding on to me out of fear, were
you?" he asked, the grin on his face wider now.

"Purely for balance."

"Uh-huh. I'll remember that when we go on the Volcano of Terror." He gestured toward a second ride that
seemed even higher and faster than the one they'd just
been on.

"You'll be screaming and holding on to *me* on that
one." She put a hand on her hip. The pool water rippled
around them in concentric waves.

"Oh, yeah? Wanna bet?"

"Sure," she said, thrusting out her hand. Then she
stopped and withdrew it. "No, sorry. I can't. This is our

only ride. I take one with each of the men and then we go back to the mansion."

Had she imagined it or was that disappointment on David's face? In the sun, the water on his chest began to dry, leaving his skin glistening and warm. For a second she longed to touch it, to put her palm against his skin again and feel the solidness of him.

But that was crazy. She didn't need him. Or his chest. Or anything else that came packaged in a guy.

"Well, if Bill or Larry isn't enough of a hero for the other rides, you know where I am." He turned and climbed out of the water, the raft bobbing along behind him.

Mattie followed. Her stomach had found her again and now it seemed a heavy thing, weighting her steps as she climbed out of the pool. This was why she didn't need to deal with men. Because all they did was send out confusing signals that she couldn't read. Put her on a soccer field and she'd be fine. But here, on a date, she was like a tourist without a map.

As Mattie took the final steps out of the pool, she glanced down at herself and realized the plunge into the water had turned the white cotton into transparent fabric.

The T-shirt had been a mistake.

Chapter Seven

The T-shirt had been a very good idea.

David hadn't been so sure he wanted to contribute to the cover-up of Mattie's amazing body. He'd been afraid, by the look in Larry's eyes, that the guys would mutiny on him if he handed over his shirt. But his mother hadn't raised him to be a jerk, so in the end, a guilty conscience and some deep-rooted sense of chivalry had kicked in like a persistent bull at his backside.

Now, though, looking at how the wet fabric clung to her body, clearly outlining the hot-pink bikini and everything else beneath it, he realized the T-shirt was a good idea. Or a bad one, depending on how he looked at the spike in his hormones and the way his gaze couldn't seem to focus on anything but Mattie as they walked back to where the others waited.

He was only interested in how that looked for the sake of the story, not personal interest.

Yeah, that was about as believable as Paris Hilton as a serious journalist.

"So, who's up for the Volcano of Terror?" David asked as they approached the next ride.

He tried not to take a perverse pleasure in the paleness of Bill's face. The other man raised both his hands and took a step back, as if warding off potential death by water slide.

"I'll go," Larry said. "I'm man enough." He grinned and lightly elbowed Mattie.

David saw her grimace and knew she hadn't liked that. In fact, he felt pretty confident she didn't like Larry at all. Maybe he'd hear "Larry" as the first name called at tonight's elimination round. Then David would be that much closer to winning the game—and Mattie's heart.

Whoa. He didn't want to win a heart here. Just the competition. And the above-the-fold front-page story that could get him back in the good graces of his editor.

But as Larry and Mattie got into line, and Larry reached out to take Mattie's hand in his own, David felt the unmistakable stab of jealousy.

Story be damned. Hell, his whole plan be damned. He'd enjoyed that water ride with her and the way she'd hid her fear. He wasn't about to let Larry have the same pleasure.

The Silhouette Reader Service™ — Here's how it works:

Accepting your 2 free books and mystery gift places you under no obligation to buy anything. You may keep the books and gift and return the shipping statement marked "cancel." If you do not cancel, about a month later we'll send you 4 additional books and bill you just $3.57 each in the U.S., or $4.05 each in Canada, plus 25¢ shipping & handling per book and applicable taxes if any.* That's the complete price and — compared to cover prices of $4.25 each in the U.S. and $4.99 each in Canada — it's quite a bargain! You may cancel at any time, but if you choose to continue, every month we'll send you 4 more books, which you may either purchase at the discount price or return to us and cancel your subscription.

*Terms and prices subject to change without notice. Sales tax applicable in N.Y. Canadian residents will be charged applicable provincial taxes and GST. Credit or Debit balances in a customer's account(s) may be offset by any other outstanding balance owed by or to the customer.

If offer card is missing write to: Silhouette Reader Service, 3010 Walden Ave., P.O. Box 1867, Buffalo NY 14240-1867

NO POSTAGE
NECESSARY
IF MAILED
IN THE
UNITED STATES

BUSINESS REPLY MAIL
FIRST-CLASS MAIL   PERMIT NO. 717-003   BUFFALO, NY

POSTAGE WILL BE PAID BY ADDRESSEE

SILHOUETTE READER SERVICE
3010 WALDEN AVE
PO BOX 1867
BUFFALO NY 14240-9952

Get FREE BOOKS and a
FREE GIFT when you play the...

LAS VEGAS
GAME

*Just scratch off
the gold box with a coin.
Then check below to see
the gifts you get!*

YES! I have scratched off the gold box. Please send me my 2 **FREE BOOKS** and **gift for which I qualify**. I understand that I am under no obligation to purchase any books as explained on the back of this card.

▲ DETACH AND MAIL CARD TODAY! ▲

© 2001 HARLEQUIN ENTERPRISES LTD. ® and ™ are trademarks owned and used by the trademark owner and/or its licensee.

310 SDL D7ZW   210 SDL D7XY

FIRST NAME   LAST NAME

ADDRESS

APT.#   CITY

STATE/PROV.   ZIP/POSTAL CODE   (S-R-12/05)

7	7	7	Worth TWO FREE BOOKS plus a BONUS Mystery Gift!
🍒	🍒	🍒	Worth TWO FREE BOOKS!
🔔	🔔	♣	TRY AGAIN!

www.eHarlequin.com

Offer limited to one per household and not valid to current Silhouette Romance® subscribers. All orders subject to approval.

"Hey, Larry," he said, coming up beside the duo. "You sure you should, ah, ride that ride?"

"I'm up for it." Larry grinned, arching his brows. "It's bigger than your ride."

"It says on the sign there that you shouldn't ride if you have a heart condition. Your ticker all right?"

Larry patted his chest. "Perfect."

Mattie eyed the two of them. Behind the trio, a girl let out a shriek as she zipped down the fast and furious Volcano's path. "You really don't need to have a he-man competition here, guys. Larry is going on this ride with me because it's his turn."

"Oh, I'm not debating whether it's his turn," David said. "Just whether it's good for his health, considering he's older than me and all."

"I'm not collecting social security yet." Larry's eyes narrowed. "Come on, Mattie, let's show this guy how it's done." He took her hand again and led her toward the inner tubes each rider picked up before climbing the long stairs.

David scowled. He should let them go alone. Those were, after all, the rules.

But when had he played by anybody's rules? That didn't get you the exclusive on the mayor's ex-wife or the shady courthouse contractor. It got you relegated to obituaries and want ads. And headlines like: Average Jill Falls in Love with Larry Herman.

Before he could think better of it, David had grabbed a raft and followed after Larry's retreating surfer shorts.

"David!" Mattie said when he caught up to them. "What are you—"

"Just want to take a trip down the Volcano," he said, cutting her off before she could object. "Anything wrong with that?"

Larry gave him a glare. "This is supposed to be my *alone* date with Mattie."

"You won't even know I'm here. I swear."

But as David headed up the stairs behind an annoyed Larry and suspicious Mattie, he wondered what a little date disrupting would do. And how it could help him get the story—and the girl—he needed.

For the rest of the day at the WaterFun Water Park, David was right behind them, glued to Mattie and Larry. Then Mattie and Bill. By the time she reached the Lazy River and Bill's time alone, Larry had realized the wisdom of David's line about "just trying out the ride" and she ended up floating along the meandering path in a quartet of inner tubes, followed by the ever-present trio of cameramen.

Alone time it was not.

Nor was it peaceful. David peppered her and the other men with questions. Either he'd become Curious George, or he had an ulterior motive.

She'd wager fifty thousand clams on the latter.

"Well, who wants to try the wave pool?" David asked. He stood in the sun, bronzed and built, seeming ten times more manly than the other two. Larry, a lawyer by trade, was pale and thin above his dark-blue swimsuit. Bill, an accountant, had a perpetual tint of green in his face, made worse by his bad experience with a blueberry snowcone at lunch.

"We're done here," Mattie said. She hadn't seen the girls from her team in the last half hour, but she wasn't about to press her luck. "You each had your time alone with me. Sort of." She eyed the trio of bachelors. All three men had perfected the who-me shrug.

"I say we do it again. Without accompaniment." Larry cast a glare David's way.

"The lady says she's done, Lar. Have a heart. You don't want to drown our bachelorette."

"I vote for the limo," Bill said. "I'm not feeling so well. I think I'm seasick."

Across Bill's head, Mattie caught David's eye. She expected to find him ready with a smart-aleck comment for Bill, but instead she found him staring at her.

With something that could only be construed as interest.

She swallowed and felt her stomach drop to her toes, the way it had when she'd reached the summit of the Tower of Chance. She glanced away, then found her gaze returning to his, as if her head were on an invisible string being pulled in his direction. When their eyes met a second time, the attraction was ten times more intense.

"That *is* Miss Grant!" she heard a voice exclaim. "I told you so!"

Dread filled Mattie's lungs. A disaster stood behind

her. And she hadn't even had to go to the Titanic Tunnel to find it.

David arched a brow at her, a question in his eyes that she wasn't going to answer.

"Let's—" But before she could get to "go," the girls were there, surrounding her in a circle.

"Miss Grant! Why are you wearing that bikini under your T-shirt?" Kelly asked first. "I thought you said you hated bikinis."

"Why are you here?" Corrine piped in at the same time.

"What's with the three guys?" Melissa asked.

That got all six of them intrigued. "Yeah, what's with the three guys?" the others echoed.

"Uh…" Mattie scrambled for something. Anything. She hadn't come up with an answer yet. Finding a way to merge feminism, hot-pink bikinis and triple-bachelor dates was out of her realm of wordplay. "Uh…"

"She's participating in the *Love and the Average Jill* reality show," David said.

Mattie shot him a glare. Nice of him to just blurt out the truth.

"No way!" The girls' jaws dropped. "*You* are on *that* show?"

Melissa punched Corrine's arm. "I told you we should have watched the first episode last night, but you wanted to watch a *Buffy* rerun."

"Hey, I didn't know Miss Grant was going to be on there. I thought it was supposed to star some beauty queen or someone equally blond and stupid." Kelly slapped a hand over her mouth. "I didn't mean Miss Grant was…well, I…"

"Now would be a good time to shut up, Kelly," Corrine said.

"I'm on the show because…" Mattie's voice trailed off. She couldn't tell them it was to raise money to start the league again. The girls had worked so hard, holding everything from car washes to bake sales, trying to come up with the funds themselves, and it still hadn't been enough. If she told them the truth, they'd feel responsible, like they had pushed her into it.

"She's here to put a new twist on those silly dating shows and prove to everyone that a woman can be athletic, smart and just as good as the men," David said. "You should have seen her last night, beating our butts at soccer."

Now why hadn't she thought of that? Had to be the lack of natural-fiber clothing and too much sun. More to the point, though, why had he? Maybe there was more to David Simpson than she'd realized.

"You did?" Kelly said.

"You rock, Miss Grant. I bet you used some killer moves." Corrine did a little jog, lifting her knees to bounce an invisible soccer ball.

"We better go, though," David said, taking Mattie by the elbow and leaning to whisper in her ear. "Before the cameramen catch up. We managed to lose them on the last turn of the Lazy River."

Then he got her out of there before the girls could ask

another question. David moved fast, keeping the lead on the cameramen and somehow losing Larry and Bill in the thick crowds.

"You didn't have to rescue me," she said to him when they reached the exit and slipped through the turnstiles.

"You looked like you needed it."

"I can take care of myself. I don't need a guy to fight my battles or open my car door. I'm perfectly capable on my own."

He stopped in the middle of an asphalt path and turned to face her. His shirt had dried on her body since they'd gotten out of the Lazy River and now it drifted about her thighs in the warm summer breeze.

"I'm sure you are, Matilda Grant. But asking for— or needing—help once in a while doesn't turn you into Rapunzel."

"And jumping in when you aren't asked to doesn't turn you into a superhero, either."

The line of his lips tightened and he lifted his jaw. "You're right. I'm not a superhero. And you don't need rescuing. I'll limit my heroics to saving Bill from becoming a water sport statistic."

Despite herself, she laughed. "You are an infuriating man."

He grinned. "We all have to be good at something." He took a step forward, coming within inches of her. The heat she'd felt earlier reappeared, ten times stronger. The crowds seemed to disappear, the world closing in to a microcosm of two. "Now you, you're good at something and you don't even realize it."

"What?"

"Driving me insane with wanting you." He reached up, pushed a stray tendril of hair behind her ear, then cupped her jaw. "Even in my clothes, you look incredible."

She swallowed. "You don't have to romance me. I'm not going to eliminate you tonight."

"And why is that?" His thumb traced the contour of her chin, slipping into the little center divot, then out again. "Am I driving you insane with desire?"

Yes. No.

His thumb slipped up, then down, mimicking the slippery ride down the Tower of Chance. Her heart doubled its beat, the sound echoing in her head.

Oh, yes.

"Not at all," she said. "I just want to keep you around so I have at least one guy I know I can beat on the soccer field."

Then she turned on her heel and headed for the exit, with as much grace as a woman in an IU T-shirt and pink sandals could possibly manage.

David and the rest of the men stood around the elaborate ballroom on the third night of *Love and the Average Jill*, all clad in tuxes and looking like penguins waiting for a spacious iceberg to open up. The camaraderie of the first few days had all but disappeared after the first two rounds of eliminations. Now they'd been reduced to caveman grunts in each other's directions while they each plotted a strategy to win Mattie.

And the money, David was sure. He knew most of the men weren't here for true love. They had other motives.

So do you, the little voice in the back of his head reminded him. Well, his case was different.

No, it isn't, and don't tell yourself it is.

The double doors were opened by the butler, and a second later Mattie strolled into the room in a ball gown, followed by Larissa and the ever present trio of cameramen. Mattie's dress, long, black and sleek, skimmed her defined frame. She walked easier in the high heels this time, her rhinestone-studded shoes making soft clicks against the hardwood floor. Her blond hair curled in soft, loose waves about her shoulders.

He hadn't thought it was possible for her to look more beautiful than she had that first night. He was finding, though, more and more often lately, that he could be wrong.

David was the first to move forward and greet Mattie. The show had kept her busy most of the day with media interviews, maybe as punishment for her ditching the cameramen at the water park, and he found he'd missed her. "You look like an angel."

"It's the makeup." Still, she smiled.

"Are you saying you're not well behaved?"

"You did see my soccer game with the topiary ball, right?"

"I'm still feeling it in my shins."

"Sorry." Her face flushed. She looked pretty like that, her cheeks brimming with the color of new apples. He found himself wondering anew if he was heading down the wrong path by chasing the Kincaid connection.

Maybe Mattie was different. More average—and less like all those other people who'd been the headliners over his career.

From behind them, music started, a classical melody piped in over the sound system buried in the walls. A waltz of some kind, David realized. Larissa hurried over, motioning to the two of them to dance.

"Apparently, we have a job to do." David put his arms in a circle and waited for Mattie to step into them.

She didn't move. "You could ask instead of thrusting out your arms and assuming I'm going to choose you as my first dance partner."

"Sorry. I think the Volcano of Terror sucked out my brains." He cleared his throat and tried again. "Will you dance with me, Mattie?"

"No."

He blinked. "No? Why not?"

"Sorry, but you have to wait your turn, Mr. Simpson." She gave him a sweet smile, then turned and crossed to the other men.

Well, he'd be damned. That's what he got for assuming things were different between him and Mattie. After the water park, he'd thought moving into the number-one bachelor slot would be a breeze.

He told himself he didn't feel one bit jealous when

she walked over to Kenny, took his hand and led him to the dance floor, leaving David's arms feeling empty.

Kenny and Mattie circled the floor, waltzing to the music. To David's surprise, Mattie was a better dancer than Kenny. Heck, than probably all of them. Maybe she had all that natural grace from playing sports. Yeah, or maybe her life as Kincaid's stepdaughter had given her more of a taste for luxury than she let on. To him it looked as if she'd been dancing waltzes all her life.

Larissa and Steve stood on the sidelines, following Mattie and Kenny with their gazes, probably to make sure Mattie didn't turn the waltz into an impromptu touch football game with the Ming vases. Larissa covered her mouth, suppressing a yawn. Steve's eyes seemed to glaze over as Mattie came around the full perimeter of the room with Kenny, then switched partners. Larissa and Steve looked as excited as toddlers at a poetry reading.

Nothing more was happening than a dance…

That was it. Nothing more was happening than a dance. Time for David to shake things up a little.

After all, one didn't get good TV or good news copy by sitting around and waiting for something to happen.

He'd just *gently* move things along.

David crossed to the couple and tapped Rick on the shoulder. "May I?"

Rick's eyes widened. He blinked a couple of times, then moved back and let Mattie go. "Uh, sure. I guess."

David smiled. "Thank you."

"What are you doing?" Mattie hissed. "I told you it wasn't your—"

"And I'm tired of letting you make all the decisions." He pressed a hand to the small of her back and spun her to one side.

"You're making the other men angry."

"Hmmm…maybe they'll riot over you."

"Oh, God, I hope not." Her face paled a few shades. Public fights over her attentions were clearly not something Mattie wanted. "You doing this kind of thing," she dipped her chin to indicate them dancing together, "isn't fair, you know."

"I'm not the kind of guy who plays by anyone's rules."

"That's something we have in common. Unless I'm in a game, I'm not much of a rule follower myself," she said.

David glanced to the side and saw Larissa wildly gesturing at Mattie to choose one of the other men. One of the cameramen panned the semicircle of men, their faces annoyed, looking like they'd step forward at any second and trample David.

"Do you even like to waltz?" he asked her.

She let out a sound of disgust. "I'd rather listen to acid rock than this."

"Well, I'll make a deal with you. I'll leave you to the other bachelors, but if the music's tempo should… change somehow, then you're mine."

Her gaze narrowed. "What are you cooking up?"

"A mutiny of sorts. But only with the musical choices."

Then he stepped back, gave her a gracious bow, and waved in Brock, the next man in line, who promptly stepped forward and elbowed past David. Brock scowled at him. "You're cheating, Simpson. We're all supposed to get equal time with Mattie."

David cocked a grin at him. "Darwin is at work, even on TV." Then he turned on his heel and started to walk away.

"What'd he mean by that?" David heard Brock mutter to Mattie.

"Survival of the fittest, apparently," she replied.

"Well, we'll see who's the fittest around here," Brock grumbled, the change in his voice telling David Brock had turned his head to make sure the competition had left the floor.

If glares were lasers, David suspected he'd have a hole the size of Texas through his back right now. Good.

All this was working into the plan.

Mattie suffered through two waltzes, rotating among the endless round of bachelors and their attempts at small talk. David had disappeared out one of the side doors. She wouldn't say she missed him...

But she sort of did. Like a cold that allowed her to call in sick to work on a rainy day.

The only man who had been remotely interesting had been Jim, who had played soccer in high school and gave her a great conversation about technique. The rest of them, though, seemed more interested in wanting to know what she did for fun: play soccer. What her favorite color was: what did it matter in the scheme of life? And whether she liked men in tuxes better than suits: neither really. She was more of a jeans and T-shirts kind of girl.

Not one of the men really asked her a question that delved into who Mattie was as a person. The whole thing felt about as personal as registering her car.

After she made her seventeenth circle around the room, the waltz suddenly cut off, followed by a second of dead air on the stereo system. Larissa looked at Steve, who shrugged his shoulders. An instant later Hootie and the Blowfish began pounding through the speakers, singing "I Go Blind."

"What the hell is that?" Jim asked.

Mattie grinned. "A gorilla, beating on his chest."

"Huh?"

"Nothing." She laughed and shook her head and when she did, she noticed David, standing in the doorway, waving a CD case for Hootie and the Blowfish's Greatest Hits back and forth. He strode forward, at the same time Steve hurried out another door, probably to find the butler and change the music back to funeral tunes.

"You owe me a dance," he said when he reached her.

"That I do." She turned to Jim. "Will you excuse me for a second?" Jim scowled but did as she asked, moving out of the way so David could take his place.

The beat of the song pounded through the parquet

floor, resonating throughout the room and echoing off its cavernous ceiling. "I Go Blind" wasn't a slow song, but it wasn't one that required fancy gyrating, either.

David had read her—and her musical tastes—perfectly.

He took both her hands and grinned. "Let's go, Miss Grant."

Excitement surged in her chest and she could feel it lighting up her face. "I thought you'd never ask."

They swung to the right, stepping as they did, in time with the rhythm. He twirled her on the harmony, then spun her back to him, her hair swinging in a wild arc. Then when she least expected it, David dipped her, one arm secure behind her back, his head coming down with hers, the movement intimate and thrilling all at once. Too soon, too fast, he scooped her up and brought her to his chest, singing along a little with Hootie's chorus. "Hold me, hold me, Mattie."

She laughed. "Seems you're the one holding me."

"You're a very holdable woman." He danced her to the right again and spun her around, circling the room in a faster pattern this time. There was no waltzing with David Simpson, just a dizzying step to the native beat that underlay the song. Mattie lost track of everyone on the sidelines; she was too swept up in David and the teasing fun in his deep-blue eyes.

She'd thought the ride down the Tower of Chance had been exhilarating and scary.

She was wrong. This was even more so.

The words of the song seemed so true, because when-

ever she looked at him, she stopped seeing the other
bachelors. She knew it was a mistake, she knew it was
distracting her from her goal, but when he had her in his
arms like this, with the rhythm of something other than
just a song running between them, she didn't want to see
anything else.

Maybe the soccer field wasn't the only place to have
fun. Who knew a dance floor and a man who looked at
her as if she were the only person in the world, could
be just as wonderful? No...better.

She laughed as he spun her again, then twirled in a
circle that ended with her back against his chest, her
head thrown against his shoulder. Mattie tipped her head
up to his, lips inches apart.

She wanted...

More of what she'd tasted that first night, that same
delicious feeling that teased between them, as elusive
as thistle blowing across a meadow.

"Hold me, hold me, David." The words came out in
a breath, half song, half request.

"I'm doing my best," he said, lowering his mouth
to hers.

Before his lips could meet her own, the song came
to an end and David pulled back. Silence once again in-
vaded the room before a bar of the next Hootie song
began. Then the CD jerked to a stop, replaced by the
godawful waltzes.

Reality was back. Reminding her that getting too
wrapped up in this fantasy world would put her in the

very place she had worked so hard to escape. She didn't belong in this girl-meets-bachelor dream. Nor did she believe David—or any of the men—was here simply to fall in love with her. If there hadn't been a price tag hanging over her head she wasn't so sure any of the men would put up with the cameras, the waltzes…any of it.

She stepped away, out of his arms. "Thanks for the dance."

"Anytime."

From across the room, Larissa's gaze was vague, not filled with disapproval, but not exactly telegraphing approval of the unwaltz, either. The bachelors, however, all had murder in their eyes. "I think you should wear full body armor when you go to bed tonight," Mattie said to David, indicating the other men.

"They already wanted to kill me the first night, when I said hello to you."

"Because it was clear that we'd already met?"

"Because it was clear there was something between us."

She may have been blind earlier, but she wasn't kidding herself now. The spell wrapped around them by the music had worn off and Mattie was back in the real world, one where men didn't find a woman's ability to block a goal kick sexy. "There's nothing between us, David, except a show. This is TV. Not life."

He took a step forward, his thumb tracing along her jaw. Everything within her reacted to his touch, but she forced herself not to let it show. "You're wrong, Mattie. There's more here than what they see on the cameras."

Out of the corner of her eye, she saw the aforementioned cameras moving in closer, going for their money shot. She looked into David's eyes and wondered whether what she read there was all about her, as he claimed. "If there wasn't fifty thousand dollars involved in this, would you be here?"

"That's not fair. It's a hypothetical question."

"Fine. Then I'll send you home tonight and we'll meet sometime at a bar or a baseball game and see if this 'magic' is real."

A shadow passed over his face, and she knew her words had hit with an arrow's accuracy. "I didn't dance with you for money, Mattie."

He hadn't said he'd danced with her because he cared about *her,* either. He hadn't denied anything she'd accused him of. As far as Mattie was concerned, she had her answer. "Maybe not, but it sure sweetens the deal, doesn't it?"

Chapter Eight

Bowden stood on the steps of the mansion and toyed with the box in his hands while he waited for someone to answer the door. He'd caught last night's episode of *Love and the Average Jill* and seen Mattie waltzing with all of the men, then, in typical Mattie fashion, breaking all the rules with David Simpson and doing a very sexy dance to a Hootie and the Blowfish song. There was definitely something between her and that man. Today Bowden hoped to help it along by giving Mattie something to show off her best assets. He'd remembered the address from when he'd switched Mattie's letter. Being a man who dealt with street numbers and zipcodes for a living came in handy sometimes.

"May I help you?" said the man who opened the door, his features so rigid, they might as well have been set in concrete.

"I have a delivery for Mattie Grant." Bowden held up the box.

Larissa Peters, the host of the show, peeked her head around the butler's tall, lean form. "A delivery? For Mattie? I think that's against the rules."

"I don't want to break any rules, ma'am," Bowden said, putting on a nice smile, "but I'd sure hate to see Miss Grant miss this. She's been waiting on this delivery for a while."

Larissa's eyes narrowed. "How did you know she was here?"

"I watched it on Lawford Channel Ten, of course."

"You're watching the show?" Larissa pushed past the butler and sidled up to Bowden's side. "Do you have a minute?"

"Well, I..." he let his voice trail off and gestured toward his green-and-white Speedy Delivery Services truck, sitting in the circular drive.

"This will just take a minute." She turned to the butler. "Find Steve. Now."

The butler pivoted, his features still unreadable, and headed into the depths of the house.

"Come in, come in," Larissa said, waving Bowden into the front room of the mansion. She gestured toward a fancy settee and asked him to take a seat. She, however, remained standing, clad in a purple satin suit and matching heels so high she teetered like a sapling on a breezy day.

Bowden placed the box on the seat beside him. "May I ask why you needed me to stay?"

A bearded man with a generous belly and a package of fries to accompany it entered the room from the opposite end. Larissa gave him a smile, then turned to Bowden. "If you don't mind, we'd like you to be a...well, a temporary focus group. Just get your impressions on the show and how Mattie Grant is faring as our Average Jill."

They wanted his opinion? Oh, he'd be glad to give that, and hopefully influence the show a little bit—in the right direction, of course.

Bowden smiled and settled back against the seat. He couldn't have created a better plan if he'd tried. True love was going to find Mattie Grant before the week was out—and if it didn't, Bowden had a lot more packages he could deliver.

It wasn't enough that they had to compete for one woman's attention every evening, but now they had to do it over bacon and eggs, too, David thought with more than a bit of grumpiness. Or rather, after their eggs, as Larissa explained. "Mattie is going to give you the rules on our next bachelor competition because she's the one who gets to go out with the winner for a romantic night for two."

Mattie stood at the head of the table, dressed in a buttercup-yellow tank, shorts and matching sandals. She looked as delicious as butter, yet the definition in her arms and legs told him she was certainly not as soft as the food.

"Since Bill, Gerry and Mark were sent home last night, we're now down to six men," Mattie began. Two of the cameramen moved in on her as she spoke, clearly not about to miss a word. A third cameraman trained his lens on the bachelors, to catch any potential reaction. David had a sudden urge to rip off his microphone and ditch the game, the reality show, the other men—all of it—and carve out his alone time with Mattie right now.

A crazy thought. The show *was* the story. And the woman, well, she just happened to be part of it.

But in the last couple of days, he'd begun to want more than the story. He'd begun to want the girl. The reporter who prided himself on staying uncommitted was suddenly becoming involved. David wasn't sure what he was going to do with all this yet, but he knew he needed to focus on work. There was safety in that, not in falling in love.

Falling in love? Where had *that* come from? Those words were enough to strike terror in his heart. He wasn't the kind of man anyone should count on for a commitment. Definitely better to refocus on work. He redirected his attention toward Mattie, purely in a non-hormonally interested-reporter way.

"Because you men seemed to enjoy the soccer game the other night and the viewers at home loved it, too,"

Mattie was saying, her smile holding a bit of self-satis-faction at being right, "the producer has decided to set up a basketball game. You'll play one-on-one until only one man is left standing. There's no elimination round tonight, just a reward for the game's winner."

David glanced at the other bachelors. A few he could beat, no problem, but there were others, like Brock, who definitely had an edge over him in the muscle de-partment. Okay, Brock had a Hulk edge.

Then his gaze traveled down the table to Mattie. For a second he felt the blaze of competitiveness in his heart, not for the story, but for her.

Whether or not his story ever got done, he was start-ing to wonder about *her* story and whether she'd ever open up enough to share it with him.

He wanted to get to know her. To see inside her heart. To find out if this soccer-playing tomboy was as golden on the inside as she seemed on the outside.

"Now. Who's game?" Mattie's eyes locked with his. If he didn't know better, he'd swear she was talking just to him.

And that made him happier than he wanted to admit.

The other men all scrambled to their feet, pushing their plates aside. "Ready when you are," Larry said.

"Good." She reached down, took off her sandals and, ignoring the cameras, tossed the shoes into a chair on the side of the room.

Then she grabbed a box off the sideboard and opened it, withdrawing a pair of red and white Adidas sneakers and white crew socks. She slipped them on, laced them, then stood again. "Now I'm ready, too."

"What are you going to do?" David asked. "Be the ref?"

She laughed. "Surely you guys know me better than that by now. I'm adding my own twist to this. Whoever wins is going one-on-one with me. And if you win that match, which I doubt you will," she gave them a smile that seemed to dare them to disagree, "I will kiss the winner."

A herd of elephants couldn't have stampeded out that door faster than six bachelors with a potential kiss on their minds.

Seeing how determined the other five men were, David prayed he was able to channel the abilities of Larry Bird in the next three minutes.

"I don't want to hear your objections," Mattie said to Larissa when the hostess reached the basketball court located on the far side of the garage. As far as home courts went, this was the deluxe version, complete with a spongy tile surface finished in navy blue and bright yellow. Clearly, the owners of the James estate were fans of their native Pacers. Even the backboard featured the team's signature yellow ball inside the letter *P*.

Brock and Jim, the first two up, were going at the game with ferocity, playing as if they had some kind of death wish for each other. For once, the cameras were focused on the men, not on Mattie.

Good thing, too. She needed some privacy and she intended to get some, whether the *Average Jill* show liked it or not. Earlier that morning she'd found the on-off switch for the microphone's battery pack. Later she'd play the on-camera game, giving Lawford Channel Ten more than its hour of nightly footage but for a few minutes, she wanted to be *off*.

"Actually," Larissa said, taking a careful seat beside Mattie on the navy wooden bench, "I wasn't going to object at all. I like how you changed the rules." She laughed and pointed at Mattie's footwear. "And your shoes."

"You do? But I thought you and Steve would have a heart attack. Figured you'd make me go back to the high heels."

"Not if those sneakers are going to help you go out there and beat some bachelor butt."

Mattie laughed, grateful for the Adidas delivery from Bowden. She had no idea how or why he'd arrived at the estate with the sneakers, but she was insanely glad not to be wearing heels for the first time in days. "That's my plan."

"You know, when you first showed up, I probably could have gotten Steve to straighten out the whole show mix-up, but then I thought—"

"Gee, wouldn't a girl who kicks the shrubbery around up the ratings?"

"No. Okay, maybe a little." Larissa flipped her long auburn hair off her neck. "I like seeing someone who isn't afraid to kick the shrubbery around. I think the women in the audience can really respect you."

Jim scored a basket and started giving himself big "hooyahs."

"Even on a show like this?"

Larissa smiled and got to her feet. "Yes, even on a show like this." She started to walk away, just as Jim scored his last basket and Larry stepped up to the court. "And, Mattie?"

"Yeah?"

"Turn your mike back on," Larissa said, pointing at the battery pack. "That's the one thing that *will* give Steve a heart attack." She waved, then walked back up to the mansion.

Mattie did as she was told, then sat back against the bench, surprised. She'd always thought the best way to influence women was by starting with the girls on her team. She'd never imagined that she could have any impact off the soccer field. Clearly, she'd been wrong.

If she'd been wrong about one thing, what else had she been wrong about?

From the opposite bench, David caught her eye and sent her a wave. The thread of connection again extended between them, across the dark-blue court. He smiled, and the thread tensed.

She realized with a start that she was beginning to like him. To look forward to seeing him in the house, at the breakfast table, at dinner.

Oh, no. That meant she was getting involved, and that

was not in the game plan. It wasn't even supposed to be on the field. She drew her gaze away, back to bachelor basketball.

Ten minutes into the game, Larry bent over at the knees, huffing and puffing. "I give," he said. "You win, Jim."

"Hooyah!" Jim punched a fist into the air, then ran a hand over his U.S. Marines issue crew cut. "Who's next?"

In short order, Jim dispensed with Kenny and Rick, leaving David as his sole competitor on the court. "Think you can beat me?" Jim asked. His cockiness, from winning every match thus far, showed on his face and in his voice.

"I intend to try." David cast a glance at Mattie, and the thread pulled taut. "I have incentive."

"So do I." Jim grinned. "As in a million-dollar kiss from a certain bachelorette."

Mattie tried not to focus on that particular outcome. She'd see who won, then deal with beating him so there'd be no kisses exchanged with anyone. Every time the word *kissing* came up, it seemed to get harder and harder to remember she was here for the Lawford Girls' Soccer League, not herself.

The two men stood at the half-court line, with Jim balancing the ball in his hands. Before they could start, David put up a hand. "How about Mattie throws out a jump ball to get us started?" He cocked his head her way and when he did, she caught the smile in his eyes.

Did he want her on the court for him...or to gain some kind of advantage over Jim?

She rose and crossed to stand between the two of them. "Sure that won't distract you?" she said, grinning at them.

"I can handle a little distraction." David stared down Jim. "Can you?"

"What distraction?" the other man said. "All I see is a ball and a man who's about to lose."

Mattie took the basketball from Jim's hands, paused a second, then tossed it up in the air. The two men leaped for the ball at the same time, but Jim was faster and higher. He had the ball out of David's hands and into his own before Mattie even had time to vacate the court.

As Jim dodged David's repeated attempts to steal the ball, Mattie tried to ignore the sinking feeling of disappointment in her stomach that told her the man who gave playing games a whole new meaning probably wasn't going to be the one she'd be eating dinner with tonight.

David hated himself for waiting outside the mansion like a worried parent with a curfew-breaking teenager. He'd played hard against Jim and had still been beaten in the stupid basketball game. That's what he got for letting his gym membership lapse in the past few weeks while he tried to salvage his job.

He could still hear Jim's victory whoops ringing in his ears. And still see Mattie leaving the mansion in a silky green dress and high heels, her arm looped through Jim's, her attention on his face....

And the sure knowledge rocketing through him that Jim would be enjoying Mattie's company, and maybe much more, for hours and hours tonight.

The only thing he was grateful for—and he'd had to look hard to find something to be happy about tonight— was that Mattie had beaten the exhausted Jim in the final one-on-one game. She'd been saved from having to give the Marine a kiss, and David had been spared watching his Mattie kiss another man.

Whoa. *His* Mattie? She wasn't his.

But, well, he *had* kissed her first. And to think of her kissing any of the other men in this house damn near tore him in two.

Which was why he was sitting on the wide granite steps, waiting for her to come back, determined to ward off a good-night kiss from Jim and hoping he'd come up with a good excuse for why he was here.

Because damn his plan to hell, Mattie Grant had started to get under his skin.

The limo came around the circular drive, twin head-lights swooshing past the landscaping and then settling on the garage.

She was home. His heartbeat quickened, and he felt a smile curve up his face.

Without waiting for the driver to open her door, Mattie got out of the car and crossed to the front steps. Alone.

David rose. "Where's Jim?"

"He ran into a couple of Marine buddies at the restaurant and stayed to chat."

Loser, David thought. He would never have done that to her. "He let you go home by yourself?"

"I'm a big girl, David. I can take care of myself." She reached down and pulled off her shoes, dangling them by their thin little straps. He could see her face visibly relax, now that the shoes were off.

A big white van screeched into the driveway behind the limo. The cameramen got out, already hoisting their equipment onto their shoulders. Mattie shook her head, clearly sick of the constant presence of the three men with their all-seeing lenses. "Guys, I'm just going to bed. Nothing else is going to happen tonight, I promise."

"Uh, we're supposed to stay with you no matter what." The first guy, whom David had dubbed Tweedledee because he looked just like one of the other cameramen, focused his lens on Mattie's face.

"You've got at least twelve hours of video of me today. Isn't that enough?"

Tweedledee looked at Tweedledum and shrugged.

"Listen, I'm beat. I know you are, too. Let's call a truce on this video thing. You guys go to bed and I promise to go to bed and not do anything that could up the ratings while you're sleeping."

"Dean, it sounds like a good idea," Tweedlethree said. He lowered the bulky equipment to his side. "I could use more than a few hours of sleep tonight."

David took a step forward, lowering his voice into a conspiratorial level and waving the trio into a confidant circle. "If you don't tell the other men I told you, I'll let you in on a secret. There's a six-pack stored in the cabana," he said. "A few of us bachelors hid it there earlier today, hoping to sneak down and drink it tonight, if we could get past the butler. But since I'm the only one who made it past the guard dog…" He put out his hands. "I guess it's up for grabs."

He could literally see their mouths water. They looked from one to the other, then at Mattie, probably weighing whether they could trust her or not. Finally the first one shrugged and took his camera off his shoulder. "All right. See you in the morning. Don't do anything I wouldn't do on video." He chuckled, then walked toward the pool house, the other two ambling along behind him.

"Is there really a six-pack?" Mattie asked when they were gone. She removed her microphone and left it on the steps.

"Yeah. I put one in there, for an opportunity just like this one."

She sighed and brushed her hair back off her face. "I appreciate it. I was about ready to offer them half the money just to leave me alone."

David laughed. "You know, I never said you weren't capable of taking care of yourself."

"Oh, yeah?" Her lips turned up in a knowing smile. "Then why were you waiting up for me?"

"I was not. I was enjoying the night air."

"Uh-huh. Out for a midnight stroll?"

"Of course."

"Good. Then let's stroll." She flipped her matching green scarf back around her neck and gestured to him to follow her. "Quietly, though, so the cameramen don't know I broke my promise."

They walked along the path that led to the gardens in the back. Wide pieces of slate were set among the grass, carving out a curved walkway. Tiny lights were tucked among the trees along their path, lighting their way with a soft yellow glow. She toyed with the scarf as she walked. "Have you always lived in Lawford?"

He hesitated. "Yeah, pretty much."

"What's that mean?"

"I've been here most of my life."

"Care to elaborate?"

"Not really."

She let out a sigh and turned to him. "You know what your big problem is, David?"

He drew up, surprised. "What?"

"You don't trust anyone."

"I trust people."

"Oh, yeah? Who? Because you sure don't trust me. Or any of the other men here."

"That's different."

"Is it?" She narrowed her gaze and stepped closer, studying him. "You want me to tell you all about myself, yet you don't want to tell me anything about you. Show me that you trust me, and I'll—" She cut herself off.

"You'll what?"

She paused, her lower lip caught in her teeth. To

David it seemed the most vulnerable gesture in the world. "I'll believe that kiss on the patio the other night was real," she said finally, her voice soft.

His chest squeezed. "It was."

"Then prove it to me."

She was asking too much of him. Asking him to open up his world and let her in. He couldn't do that. He'd blow his cover, and...hell, he didn't let anyone in. Trusting people was what got him in trouble. Hadn't he learned that lesson a hundred times over in his job? "How do you want me to prove it? You want me to tell you my shoe size? Ten and a half. My favorite color? Blue. I grew up in Lawford, an only child of divorced parents. That's my personal résumé, in a nutshell."

She shook her head. "That's not what I want—some rundown of who you are, like a menu at a fast food joint. I mean real trust." She paused a minute and in that time, David worried what she meant by "real" trust. He hadn't had that with anyone in such a long time, he wasn't sure he could go along with whatever she said next.

"There's something I do at the beginning of the season with my teams to build trust among them," Mattie said. "We always have at least a couple of new girls, so this trust exercise helps the whole team get to know each other."

"You aren't going to kick anything into my shins again, are you?"

"No." She laughed, reaching up to pull the scarf off her neck. "But I would like to try what we call a 'trust walk.'"

"A trust walk?"

"I put this over your eyes and lead you around. You have to trust me, and listen to the sound of my voice. If you do, then you don't walk into anything. If you don't, well…I hope you have cranial insurance."

"You want to blindfold me, and I'm supposed to trust you not to walk me off a cliff?"

"Exactly. Besides, there are no cliffs at the James Estate. We are in Indiana, you know." She twisted the scarf, then raised it toward him. "Are you game?"

The echo of his own words triggered the adventurer in him. He couldn't say no. Not to that kind of challenge and especially not to those eyes and that smile. "Of course." He turned around, bent down a little and allowed her to tie the scarf around his head. In an instant the world went black.

"Now, take my hand," she said.

With his vision gone, David's sense of touch became ten times more sensitive. Mattie's palm felt softer. More delicate. Worry about trust disappeared and fantasies about her palm on other parts of his body raced through his mind. He wanted to kiss her, to pull her to him, to forget walking anywhere at all.

But she had other plans.

"Move forward, five steps," Mattie said.

He did as he was told, his movements hesitant at first, then more confident as she walked with him, her hand holding his tightly and securely. He tamped down the oddness of being the vulnerable one, the man under the woman's control, and allowed her to tell him to turn right, take three steps, then left and take five more.

He could hear the calls of night birds, the crackle of a branch, the screech of a bat overhead, the whisper of the wind. But most of all, he was aware of Mattie. Her perfume. Her touch. Her sweet voice, carrying across the night air and straight into him.

"Bend your head a little, about down to chin level. There's a branch right in front of you."

He did as he was told, and as he moved forward, the sensation of the tree limb lightly brushed the top of his head but didn't bump him. "Now what?"

"We're in the gardens and we're rounding the first corner. There's a bench up ahead. If we get to that, we'll see what kind of trust we have."

"What do you mean?"

"We have to skirt the koi pond to get there."

"I hope I didn't do anything to make you mad today," he joked.

She paused a second, the moment seeming longer without his vision. "Not at all."

He paused, then decided to hell with it. He had to know. "Did you kiss him?"

"Who?"

"Jim."

She didn't answer and David thought he'd go insane. Not being able to see meant he couldn't read her body language. He didn't know if she was stalling, concentrating on something else, or just avoiding the truth.

His hand went to the blindfold, to rip it off and find out what that silence meant.

Before he could, she grabbed his other hand. The sandals in her grasp swung against his knuckles. "We're at the koi pond. You need to really listen to me so you don't trip on the edge. Just follow my voice and move forward with me."

He took small steps toward her. The water gurgled beside them, and a small splash signaled either a fish or a frog running from human presence. Beneath his feet, the stone perimeter felt hard. "Did you?"

"Why do you want to know?"

"Because…"

What could he tell her? Because it made him insane to think of her kissing anyone else? Because he wanted to be the only bachelor she was involved with?

That was impossible. He'd seen these shows on TV. The whole purpose was to get the bachelorette to try out as many of the men as possible. That was surely her goal, too, to give each of the men a whirl before picking one. A clump of jealousy clogged up his gut.

"Because you're starting to like me?" Mattie asked when he didn't finish, still leading him along the side of the pond.

"Aren't you supposed to be helping me stay dry instead of asking me about feelings?"

"This is all about trust, David. I'm asking you because I want to trust you."

He swallowed. Answering her question would mean

opening himself up to her. He hadn't done that with anyone in years. Too many times he'd trusted someone with his heart and realized too late that it had been a mistake.

He'd be the one taking the chance here. Mattie hadn't answered his question. He had no idea what had gone on during that date with Jim. All he knew was that she had come home alone and was now out in the gardens with him, leading him blindfolded like a cow to the slaughter.

Or a man to his destiny. Whatever that might be.

"You're past the pond. You're on grass again," Mattie said. "The bench is right behind you. If you sit, you'll be done with the trust walk."

He lowered himself, half expecting to hit the ground, but finding instead the smooth marble seat beneath him as she'd promised. Mattie released his hands. They were done. Disappointment joined the mishmash in his stomach.

David tugged off the scarf and handed it to her. His eyes took a second to adjust to the moonlight, but when they did, he found her staring at him, waiting for an answer.

He had a job to do. And that job didn't involve trusting her or opening up his heart. In the end, he was sure he'd find something rotten about Mattie Grant, just as he had about every other person he'd ever interviewed, and whatever trust he'd had in her would be gone. Better to avoid that now by keeping his heart out of the equation. "Of course I'm starting to like you, Mattie," he said with a smile that felt fake. "You're the most likable bachelorette in Lawford."

Hurt shone in her face, and for a moment David wondered if his instincts, which he'd once prided himself on, had been wrong this time. Maybe she *was* the real deal and he was too jaded to see it.

"I guess trust doesn't come easily to you, does it?" she said. "You can't even tell me what you're feeling right now."

She was right. Five seconds ago he'd had a scarf over his eyes, his world comprised of nothing but Mattie's voice and her words. He'd trusted her then and she hadn't steered him wrong or into the koi pond, and he was sure he deserved at least one dunking with the goldfish. Would it be so bad to see where she led him now?

He dropped his head and let out a breath. "I haven't met many people I can trust."

"I think that's pretty sad, David. But it's something I understand, in a way."

He studied her, his memory dropping into place the pieces he'd found. Losing her father at an early age. The corrupt stepfather. The stepsister who'd married three times. A mother who lived on the other side of the country. "Really?"

She swung her legs against the bench, her bare feet swishing along the grass. "I grew up in a family where money was everything. Status. Clothing. Cars. But not love. My stepfather cared about how the family looked on the outside but not about the inside, where it counted. We didn't have a family, we had a status in society. When he divorced my mother, all of the money, status, everything was taken away from her. She was devastated. It took her years to get over what Stephen Kincaid did to her. Hell, I think it took both of us years." She drew the scarf between her hands, coiling it around her fingers. "I learned early on that some lifestyles come with a price tag. One I don't want to pay. So I went out on my own at eighteen and haven't relied on anyone else since. If the league didn't need so much to get it started again, you can bet I wouldn't be here."

Here was the story, the details he'd been seeking. All he had to do was push a little more and he could have that headline. He opened his mouth and asked the question he knew he had to ask, hating himself as the words left his mouth. "Why did the league get into such financial trouble?"

"That little trust issue." She shook her head, the disgust evident in her features. "Seems I have one, too. I dated a man who was a backer for the league. You'd think I'd know better. Conflict of interest and all that. When I turned out not to be the kind of woman he wanted, meaning I didn't put on *this* kind of stuff on a regular basis—" she gestured toward the dress and swung the heels a little "—he dropped me and the league sponsorship. Turned out he was looking for a little eye candy, not anything real. He'd never loved me. Not the real me, anyway."

He heard the hurt and disappointment in her voice and knew what the man had done to her. Then he realized how *he'd* done the same thing with that dinky three-paragraph story he'd written on her league. He'd given her and the league short shrift, tossing them aside for front-page eye candy. When he got back to work, to the real world, he vowed to make up for it.

"But now you're putting on this stuff again to regain the money for the league?"

"Yeah, but it's on my terms and it's my choice. And it's only for a week, not a lifetime." She grinned. "Trust me, I'll be back in my cleats soon and out of Hermès." She flicked the scarf at him.

He caught the tail of it and tugged it, and her, closer to him. "And out of all of our lives at the end of this?"

"Back to my job at least. I have a league to run."

"You have a right to a love life, too."

"That's what my friend Hillary says. But all that can wait. The girls need me more."

The scarf slipped out of her grasp and David raised it to caress the side of her cheek, silky fabric against soft skin. "Maybe you're not trusting what's in your heart. Should we try tying this on you?" He drifted the Hermès over her face, fluttering it across her eyes.

Heat teemed with the double meanings hanging in the air. Her emerald eyes caught his. He could see her emotional tug-of-war between want and need.

"I can't," Mattie said, suddenly jerking to her feet. "I'm not here to fall in love."

She was going to leave, run back to that mansion and distance herself from him all over again. If he were smart, he'd let her go. But something had changed in those moments when he'd been blindfolded, and he didn't want things to go back to the way they'd been.

Some intangible need David had been missing for years felt as if it was right there, just out of his grasp, waiting for him to push through the door and see it. His heart and his mind told him Mattie was the key to that door.

"Neither am I," he said, "but sometimes it happens when we're not looking." He rose and caught her hand in his. "You never answered my question. Did you kiss him?"

She shook her head.

"Why?"

"Because…" Mattie looked toward the trees, as if deciding whether to open up to him, then turned back. "Because he didn't win the one-on-one."

Then she turned and went back to the mansion, the hated high heels swinging from her fingers, and the answer to the most important secret still tucked inside.

Chapter Nine

They were down to four.

In last night's live circus-on-camera ceremony, Mattie had eliminated two more bachelors, leaving the quartet of Larry, Kenny, Jim and David.

And worse, it was Wednesday. The week was nearly over and David had yet to come up with anything to write about. Actually, he had plenty to write about—the links to Kincaid, the rich girl turned soccer coach, the former debutante who preferred cleats over tiaras—but what he lacked was the desire to put a single word on paper.

Carl wanted something on his desk today by five so he could splash it across the *Lawford Sun*'s morning edition.

And David had nothing.

Nothing but a mind full of thoughts of what Mattie Grant had felt like in his arms and a conscience that seemed bound and determined to ruin his career.

He tucked the laptop away in its case, left the room and headed downstairs. Mattie stood there in a fitted black and pink sundress with matching strappy shoes, a pink floral tote bag slung over one shoulder. She looked ready for a garden party…

Or a kiss.

He halted on the landing before the last few stairs and decided to ramp up his game. Not just because of the deadline hanging over his head but because—

Because looking at her standing there, smiling at him, did something funny to his gut that he hadn't thought he would ever feel. And like the first breath of spring after a long winter, he didn't want to let it go. Not at the end of today. Not ever.

"Good morning," he said, heading down to meet her. "What's on our agenda today?" They'd spent the last few days in group activities. He supposed all those multiple bachelor dates had been designed to encourage jealousy and spark a few ratings-worthy squabbles as they neared today, the final day of the show.

Even outside the group dates, though, Mattie had avoided David since the koi pond incident, sticking with the other men during social times and taking solo walks whenever they weren't engaged in events for the show. He'd found he missed her, not just her voice but also her presence.

"There is no agenda for you and me." She shook her head. "I'm off to the zoo with Larry, Kenny and Jim for their alone dates. You already had yours at the water park. Have to give everyone a fair chance, you know."

Fair chances be damned. He didn't have time for those. And…if he were honest with himself for five minutes, he'd admit he couldn't stand the thought of her spending time with anyone but him. "What if you don't go?"

"What? I have to. They're doing a live elimination of the next two men at noon, then the big finale tonight with the final two. I can't skip out on this."

"Says who?"

"Says the contract I signed that says I'll abide by the rules of the show."

"And these 'rules' *make* you go out alone with the other men? Did it have that specifically in your contract?"

"Well…no."

"Then I rest my case." He grinned. "Play hooky. And go somewhere with me today."

She put a hand on her hip. "Where?"

Yeah, Bennett, where? He'd come down these stairs without a plan, just an overwhelming desire to be with her. He scrambled to come up with something Mattie would enjoy more than a trip to the zoo with three men who'd spend the entire day falling all over themselves to flatter her.

"What if I told you I could get you in to batting practice with the Lawford Trawlers?"

"The baseball team? But I heard the batting practices were closed to the public."

He grinned. "They're closed to people who don't have connections." He had connections—in the sports editor at the *Lawford Sun* who owed David a favor for not printing a word about a particularly embarrassing DWI with a redhead and a shaker full of martinis.

Her eyes were bright with excitement, her face awash with the thought of what was to come for the day. Then David saw it all drain away. "I shouldn't. I'm supposed to—"

"I bet the team members would really love to come talk to the girls on your league some time. Give them some pointers on how to make it to the pros. I know it's not a soccer team, but they've been through the ups and downs like other pros have. And it would be one more way to spread the word about girls' soccer."

She considered him for a long moment, clearly weighing the consequences. He realized that, when it came to her league, Mattie didn't act without thinking.

"Mattie?" Larissa's voice carried down the long hallway. "Are you ready? Your bachelors are waiting to go monkey seeing with you."

"My car's out back," David said, withdrawing the keys and dangling them in front of her. "Monkeys or baseball players?"

"You promise me an autograph from Darren Williams, the pitcher, and I'll go."

"Anything you want, Mattie," David said, taking her

hand and making a mad dash for the back door. "Anything at all."

If he'd had any objectivity left when he woke up this morning, it was gone now. The story had become personal. And that presented a problem bigger than the Tower of Chance.

No microphones. No cameras. No bachelors.

Well, no bachelors except for David.

Mattie felt freer than she had in days. A twinge of guilt hit her as she heard the back door of the house close behind her, but she pushed it away. She'd felt that when she'd left home at eighteen, too, but in the end, it had been the best choice she'd ever made.

She probably could have stuck it out—it was the last day after all—but the thought of spending twelve more hours with those cameras glued to her every move made hang gliding *without* the glider look more fun. She was so close to the money. Walking out might be crazy, but she was sure that when she returned she could smooth the waters with the producer and make everything work out. But for now, for just a minute, she needed a break.

"I think it's too late to worry about getting into trouble," Mattie said as she slipped into the passenger's side seat of David's Taurus.

He turned to her and smiled. "We were in trouble from the first day."

Wasn't that the truth? Meeting David had triggered something inside her that she'd thought she didn't need.

She'd been wrong.

As they zipped out of the mansion's driveway, Mattie saw Larissa standing on the granite steps, shouting and waving at them to come back. "Want to turn around?" David asked. "It's your last chance."

She thought of the day ahead with three men she barely knew. Another one of those farces put on for the cameras. She was risking the fifty thousand, but she was also potentially going to make enough contacts at the Lawford Trawlers to make up for that.

And besides, as long as she fulfilled her end of the bargain and chose a man, the show couldn't keep the money from her. She'd made a deal—and she'd keep it. Later.

A bunch of bachelors vying for every second of her time…or freedom and a few curve balls. The choice was easy.

"Put some lead behind that gas pedal, Simpson," she said.

David happily obliged. They zipped along the quiet residential road, his Taurus handling the curves like a marble along a Matchbox track. Mattie rolled down her window, enjoying the feel of fresh summer air against her face. That was where she belonged—outside and in the sun, not cooped up in some fancy house wearing designer duds and self-curling mascara.

Fifteen minutes into their escape, a bell dinged and a yellow light appeared on the dashboard display. David let out a curse. "I'm out of gas."

She snorted. "Yeah, right. That line hasn't worked on a girl in twenty years."

"No, really, I am. I have a sticky gas gauge. Sometimes it doesn't say it's empty—" the car began jerking and coughing, then sputtering to a slow, shuddering stop "—until it is. All the way."

"Didn't you think to fill it before you arrived at the mansion a week ago?"

"I didn't expect to be making a break for it on the last day."

She shook her head. "I thought Boy Scouts taught young men to be prepared for every contingency?"

A shadow seemed to pass over his face. "I was never a Boy Scout."

Once again David was keeping everything about himself locked away. Mattie had hoped he would open up to her before the end of the show. But he'd yet to tell her much of anything. What was he keeping hidden?

And more important, why? Was he, as she suspected so many of the men she'd sent home already had been, here only for the money?

David got out of the car and slipped the keys into the pocket of his khaki shorts. Mattie slid out and locked the door before coming around to where he stood, waiting for her, at the front of the now silent car.

"Hold on a minute," she said, hoisting her tote bag onto the hood of the car. "I'm not exactly ready for a long hike here."

"Not in those shoes you aren't." He grinned. "I do like them, though."

"Apparently so do the viewers." Mattie rolled her eyes. "Larissa told me this morning that the biggest concentration of viewer e-mail to the show's Web site has been about my shoe choices."

"What came in second?"

"The man the viewers think I should choose at the end of all of this."

"And who's in the running?"

"Well," she hesitated, unzipping the top of her bag, "you."

"Me?"

"You've got a good LFQ, according to Larissa."

"LFQ?"

"Lawford Female Quotient." Mattie withdrew her Adidas running shoes from the bag, set them on the ground, then removed her sandals. "Apparently you're a hit with the ladies."

He moved to stand beside her. Hot air emanated off the car's hood, filling the centimeters of space between them. Birds chirped in the woods, crickets sang their songs, and from somewhere far away, Mattie could hear the hum of a highway.

"All of them?" David asked.

His hand rested on the hood of the car, a few inches from her own. All she'd have to do was reach, and he'd be there, his palm against hers, his fingers grasping hers. It would be so easy.

So tempting.

Her mind was rocketed back to the moment on the water slide, the solidity of his hand in hers as they made their way up to the ride, the feel of his back against her cheek. Like someone she could depend on, lean on once in a while.

Then Mattie thought of how he'd refused to open up, no matter how hard she'd tried to get to know him. She jerked her hand away, bent down and started putting on her sneakers. "I don't think *every* woman in Lawford watches *Love and the Average Jill*, as much as the producers wish they would."

"I don't care about every woman in Lawford," he said, bending to his knees beside her. He tipped her chin so she was forced to look at him. Her hand paused in the middle of tying the bow. "I care about *your* opinion."

"Why are you really here, David?"

"To win."

"Me? The money? Or something else?"

"There is nothing else." A shadow flickered in his eyes.

"Somehow I don't believe you." She finished the first lacings, then switched feet and started tying the other shoe. It was easier to concentrate on a perfect set of bunny ears for her sneakers than to look into his eyes and read the truth. She was suddenly afraid that if she saw he was after monetary gain, she'd dissolve onto the hot tar like a lonely raindrop.

"You think I have an ulterior motive for being here?"

"Doesn't everyone? I mean, I do. I'm here for the league, not for myself." She got to her feet, both shoes tied now, and dusted off imaginary road dirt from her skirt.

He took the opportunity to move closer to her, to invade her personal space and increase the temperature in the already heated, flower-scented summer air. "You aren't here for love? Not even a little bit?"

A little bit? Heck, how about a lot, if she were honest with herself. How long had she been a solo act, confiding to no one but Hillary about her real feelings, wants and needs? And even then, she'd mostly left her best friend in the dark.

Mattie Grant had perfected the art of pouring herself into her work. And now without the league to keep her busy, those hours seemed to stretch ahead of her, lonely, unfulfilled.

But not so unfulfilled that she was ready to take a chance on a man she didn't entirely trust.

"I'm not looking for love," she said, snatching the sandals off the hood of the car, if only to have something to occupy her hands. "Just…"

"What, Mattie? What?" David moved closer, placing one hand against her face, cupping her cheek in a gesture so soft she almost believed he cared.

"Just…"

And then she couldn't talk any more because David's face was moving toward hers and her lips were tingling with the anticipation of his kiss. She didn't want him…and she did.

Desire won out. Mattie stopped thinking and simply acted. She dropped her sandals to the ground and wrapped her arms around his back, the soft cotton of his shirt like a comforting blanket.

David's mouth opened against hers, and his tongue darted in, tasting her. A rocket exploded in her midsection, carrying want and need through every vein of her body, like a trail of fire. The feel of him zipped up her internal scale from comfort to desire, and then to something so foreign and strong she fought the urge to run from it and run into it at the same time.

David's hands cupped her face, his thumbs resting in the hollows of her cheeks. She felt treasured, craved. Mattie pressed herself to him, finding an answering reaction in David's body.

Never had she been kissed like this. Never had a man poured his whole self into such a simple thing, never had anyone made her feel more like a woman. Even if she was wearing a Liz Claiborne dress and Adidas sneakers.

His hands drifted to her breasts, thumbs trailing over the nipples. Desire spiked inside her and she arched against him, her pelvis pressing to his, wanting, asking, needing…. Anything. Her breath left her, then whooshed back in like a tornado in her chest.

Their kiss deepened, the heat of the day and of everything between them intensifying every moment. She moaned and tangled her hands in his dark hair, melding the rest of her against his hard length.

He drew back slowly, ending with a sweet, perfect kiss on her lips. "I hope that raised my MQ."

"Your MQ?" She had no idea what the hell he was talking about. Heck, she had no idea what day it was right now.

He grinned. "My Mattie Quotient."

"Oh, I think you got a point or two." Mattie worked on recovering some oxygen.

"That's all? I better try harder next time."

"Next time." The words both scared and excited her. To anticipate more…and yet to know it was coming meant opening doors she'd left shut for so long.

"We should, ah, get going before they send out the search-and-rescue dogs to find us."

"Yeah, you're right." That was probably a good idea. Wasn't it?

David released her and stepped back. "But first, tell me about the shoes. You're the only woman I know who carries running shoes in her purse."

She laughed, glad for the joke and the way it eased the simmering, twisting tension between them. "They were a delivery."

"A delivery?"

"Larissa said my Speedy Delivery Services guy came by the mansion and dropped them off. He told her I ordered them, but I don't remember it. There wasn't a packing slip or anything, and I was sick to death of high heels, so I didn't question it. I figured I'd worry about whether it was a misdelivery later."

"Maybe the SDS guy has an ulterior motive." David arched a brow at her shoes. "Perhaps he wants you to run away with him."

She laughed again. "That is the worst pun I have ever heard."

"That's why I don't make my living as a comedian."

Mattie picked up her sandals, dropped them into her tote and swung it over her shoulder, grateful to be back to their usual banter. It was a lot easier to trade jokes with him than kisses, which took her into unknown territory. "What *do* you do? You didn't mention a job when you were introduced."

"I spend my days rescuing pretty damsels from fire-eating reality shows. Now, let's get going before you miss batting practice and the opportunity to throw a fast ball at Lawford Park."

As she fell into step beside David, Mattie pressed a finger to her lips, still tingling with the feeling of his kiss.

Maybe making the title of the show come true wasn't such a bad idea after all.

David toyed with the autographed baseball in his hands as the two of them walked out of the park and toward a diner a few blocks down the street. He hadn't had this much fun in ages. Not that he'd taken batting practice with the Lawford Trawlers—he might as well have been a pile of compost the way the guys ignored him the instant they saw Mattie—but still, the day had been great.

Actually, what had been great had been watching

Mattie. Her smile. Her laughter. Her power swings at the ball, despite wearing a dress and sneakers. Then to hear the crack of her bat…

It had told him she wasn't an ordinary woman.

Hell, he knew that the minute she'd hiked up her skirt and kicked a topiary ball at his shins.

"Do we have to go back?" she asked.

"Eventually."

"You still want to play hooky?" She spun on the sneakers and lifted her face to the sun. "Because I can't face that mansion right now."

"I take it you're not an indoors kind of girl."

She shook her head and circumvented a *Lawford Sun* newspaper dispenser on the sidewalk. David looked away, trying not to imagine the headline that was supposed to blare from that bright-blue container tomorrow.

"Not at all," Mattie said. "Never have been much for the indoors, never will be."

"I used to love to be outdoors, before I got stuck in a desk job."

Oh, damn. He'd let that slip. He'd tried so hard not to talk about his work, even cleverly avoiding her earlier question, but now he'd gone and reintroduced his job into the conversation.

"A desk job would be the death of me," she said. "I tried it once and lasted two whole days as a receptionist at Ricker's Heating and Air-Conditioning."

He laughed. "Two whole days. I bet that was a lot for you."

"I was desperate for a check. I'd just left home and took the first job that came along."

"My first job was sorting T-shirts in a warehouse."

"Ooh, sounds exciting."

"It was, later, when the owner was arrested for trafficking drugs in the T-shirt boxes."

"Really? Did you know?"

"I put the pieces together eventually," he said, leaving out the details. That first job had led to his current job because he'd seized the opportunity to tell the editor he'd give him the inside scoop on the warehouse—if he gave David a chance as a writer. Carl had laughed, but brought in seventeen-year-old David, anyway.

And kept him on. Ever since David had discovered that first deception, he'd made a name for himself uncovering lies. A name that would be in jeopardy if he didn't keep his focus on the story here—instead of the girl. He glanced at the afternoon sky and realized his five-o'clock deadline was nearing.

It was time to make a decision. Write a story about Mattie that would hit the three hundred thousand copies of the *Lawford Sun* or hit the unemployment line.

"So, what do you do now? I assume you didn't make a career out of exposing T-shirt traffickers." She grinned.

If only Mattie knew how close she'd come. "I write poetry, remember?"

"No one makes a living at that."

"Only the truly great ones do." He gave her a smile

and took her hand with his. His chest tightened and his heart felt as if someone was shredding it a little at a time.

She wasn't in an inquisitive mood, thank goodness, and gave his palm a playful squeeze. "How do you know you're great?"

"Same way you know when a kick is going to go in the goal and when it won't. Instinct."

"Luck is more like it." She laughed.

He took in her heart-shaped face, so vibrant and full of life. The complete opposite of him, she was a woman who lived life with gusto, who took on challenges and kicked butt. So many years of uncovering lies and he'd yet to find anyone as golden as her.

"And are you feeling lucky now?" he asked, pausing on the sidewalk with her.

"Are you going to start reciting verse?"

"No. Not at all." Then he moved forward, broke his own rules and kissed her again.

She was honey in his arms, sweet and warm, and a craving he couldn't satisfy. David had dated a lot of women in his life, but none had been quite like Mattie Grant. They all seemed…lacking somehow, as if they were too much like him. Too jaded, too worn by everything around them.

Who would have thought that he would meet a woman like her on the most jaded type of television there was—reality TV?

"You keep that up, and we'll never get back to the mansion," Mattie said when they came up for air.

"Now that's an idea," he said, considering it as much for himself as anything else. Run away. That was a thought. Not a good one, but hell, he didn't have many options right now. "You did, after all, get some great commitments from the team. I loved their idea of holding an autographing benefit for the girls' league."

"That is going to help. But if I want to keep the league running, I still need the fifty thousand. so I have to get back some time today and finish this up."

He brushed back a tendril of long blond hair that had fallen across her eyes. "Are you for real, Mattie?"

"I hope so." She smiled.

"I'm serious. I never meet people like you."

"What do you mean, people like me? I'm no one special. Just a soccer coach, trying to get a league back up and running."

"There, like that. You say it like it's nothing."

She shrugged and blinked at him. "It *is* nothing, David. I'm the average Jill, remember?"

"Not in my world." He started walking again, tossing the baseball up and catching it in his palm.

Mattie's hand darted in and snatched the ball midair. "Not so fast. I detect some hidden issues there. We have a long walk back, why not talk about them?"

"Trust me. You don't want to hear my long sad story."

She let out a gust of frustration. "How do you know I don't want to hear it if you won't tell me?"

"Because it's one of those stories everyone's heard a million times. Besides, I'm all grown-up now, handsome as hell—" he grinned, hoping the joke would change the subject "—and no longer blaming my bad habits on my parents."

She handed him back the baseball. "Fine."

"No pop quiz? No more questions?" He should have been grateful she'd let it go, but in some strange, masochistic way he wasn't.

"You know, I grew up in a life I hated. It's not my favorite subject. So I won't press you if you don't press me."

"And neither one of us gets to know the other, is that it?"

Now that he'd spoken the words aloud, the reality of them hit home. That wasn't what David wanted. Not anymore.

His gaze connected with Mattie's and he decided the unemployment line was something he could live with. What he couldn't live with was waking up in the morning knowing he had hurt her. Tonight, he vowed, after he had a chance to talk to Carl and substitute some other story for Mattie's, he'd tell her the truth. Come clean, and hope like hell she'd let him start all over again.

Because she wasn't a story to him anymore. She was a woman he was falling in love with.

She swallowed and took several steps before answering. "Yeah, I guess so."

"And in the end you get to keep both the fifty thousand and your heart. Am I right?"

She put on a phony smile. "That's the plan."

David stopped in the middle of the sidewalk. "My

plan was something similar, but it isn't anymore. I thought I knew what I wanted when I started on this show, but I was wrong."

She exhaled a sharp breath. "You wanted the money, right?"

"No. There was something else." He wanted so badly to tell her now, but knew if he didn't give Carl something else first, his editor might run the story himself and in the end, Mattie would still be hurt. David needed a chance to make it right before everything went wrong. "I know I'm not giving you much here, but if you can just trust me for a few hours, I'll tell you everything."

"Trust you? David, I barely got to know you this week."

"Mattie, I might not have talked about my job or where I grew up, but this week you got to know me better than anybody else in my life." He paused as a crowd of businesspeople, discussing lunch options, passed between them. "I'm a man who thought he'd lived, seen and knew it all until I met you." David took her hand, splaying Mattie's fingers in his own and tracing over them, memorizing the feel of her palm against his. "I realized I only saw half the world, maybe the wrong half. Or maybe my vision was cloudy. I saw other people with the white-picket-fence life and I thought it was all a crock, figuring they had to be hiding something, some weeds in that perfect lawn. But now—" he closed his palm over hers "—I've begun to believe again that maybe there *are* perfect lawns and pretty fences out there."

She shook her head. "Nothing's perfect, David. You just take what you can get. You battle the weeds, keep on putting down grass seed every year and hope for the best."

He smiled. "See? That's what I like about you. You're a realist, but an optimist, too. You make me remember who I wanted to be years ago."

Her eyes filled with confusion. "Who you *wanted* to be? Who are you now?"

"I don't know," David said. "But I'm trying to figure it out. If you can wait just a little bit—a few hours—I'll tell you. But I can't right now. I need time."

She took a step away, breaking their connection. "I don't know. I'm not sure what to believe."

He caught up with her, thrust the baseball into her hand and closed her palm around the white surface, fingers brushing against the red stitching. "Everything between us this week was real, believe me. As real as this ball. *This* is tangible and lasting, Mattie."

Then he took her in his arms and quieted the little voice in his head that told him he was doing her more harm than good, saying, "And so is this," just before kissing her.

Chapter Ten

"Where is the Average Jill?" the newscaster blared, cutting into the middle of a soap opera broadcast. "Lawford Channel Ten's Average Jill, Mattie Grant, has gone missing today. The producers have issued a photo and a description…" The picture Mattie had sent in with her *Survival of the Fittest* application popped up on the screen, along with all the particulars about her body running along the bottom, like the pricing on a package of chicken thighs. "…hoping someone will have seen their Average Jill and bring her back to the mansion and her waiting bachelors." At this, the image of the other three remaining bachelors, lolling about in chairs on the lawn, looking woeful and lonely, was shown.

What had she done? She'd thought she could sneak

away unnoticed. Apparently Lawford Channel Ten didn't wait long to put out an APB on missing reality-show contestants.

"Seems we were missed," David deadpanned, gesturing toward the television with his fork. They sat in a diner down the street from the Lawford Trawlers baseball park, eating cheeseburgers and French fries with cole slaw on the side. It had been the perfect ending to a perfect day.

A day that had left Mattie feeling a little disconcerted. After all this time of not opening up, David had given her a mystery…and kisses that left no doubt he cared about her. She found herself looking forward to tonight, to whatever he had to tell her.

"Just a little," Mattie said, laughing. "At least they used the picture that shows my good side."

The newscaster continued with the report, running clips from the past two days. Oh God, there she was in the tiny pink bikini, before she'd convinced David to give her his shirt.

"I do like your swimwear choices," David said.

"You would." She shook her head and went back to listening, with a sense of impending doom building in her stomach.

The wonderful day with David was over. She had to go back. Had to face the men waiting for her, and the choice she'd ultimately have to make.

"Mattie left with one of the bachelors, a man calling himself David Simpson."

Mattie's breath left her. She stared at the screen,

watching the words come out of the newscaster's mouth, but not believing the sounds she heard.

Calling himself.

Pretending to be.

Not really…

"…but he isn't who he claimed, says the producer of the reality show. It turns out the real David Simpson is alive and well and on vacation with his girlfriend in Lake Tahoe."

Mattie glanced at David, but something blurred her vision. He reached for her hand, but his touch no longer held the power it had five minutes ago. "Let me explain, Mattie."

She jerked away from him and got to her feet. "I don't want to hear anything you have to explain."

"But—"

"But nothing."

He'd lied. Everything that had come out of his mouth had been a lie.

"Tune in tonight," the newscaster continued, her voice high and excited, "when we see what happens when the true identity of this bachelor is revealed to Mattie and we see if sparks fly…or a love connection is made on *Love and the Average Jill*."

"Oh, I already know the answer to that," she muttered to herself.

Diners pivoted on their seats to look at her. It took a millisecond for them to connect Mattie's real-life face with the TV version. "Isn't that…?"

"I watched her last night…"

"She's out with one of them now…"

"We should call…"

And then, cutting through the undertow of murmuring voices, David's insistent one. "Mattie, please let me explain."

She had to leave. Now. Before anyone else recognized her. Or worse, she began to listen to David's justifications for breaking her heart.

"How could you? You used me. You lied to me." She withdrew some bills from her tote bag and tossed them at the table. "And I'm not letting you do it ever again."

She turned and ran for the door, heading for the one person in the world she could trust to have a sympathetic ear and a fast ride out of this mess.

"Hey, look at it this way, at least you're famous," Hillary said later over a pint of Cherry Garcia ice cream. Mattie had dashed down to Hillary's office at the Lawford Insurance Company after the public and devastating debacle with David. She'd been able to keep the tears in check, but the hurt had clearly shown on her face.

Hillary, as only a best friend could, had immediately taken a half day off, claiming a sudden migraine, and secreted Mattie out the back door, into her Honda Civic and over to her apartment in the Lawford historic district. The Pierpont Building, a converted factory that had been renovated as part of a push to beautify the older areas of the city, held five dozen apartments, each unique in their layout because of the building's nooks and crannies.

Hillary lived on the third floor; Mattie lived on the fourth. The plan had been to bring Mattie home—until they'd seen the TV and newspaper reporters camped out in the stairwell between the two floors. Now, they were pretty much stuck in Hillary's apartment.

Good thing she had a big stock of Ben & Jerry's. Mattie needed that and a heck of a best friend right now.

"Yeah, famous for being duped," Mattie said.

"There are worse things in life."

"I didn't even get the money because I didn't return to finish the last day." She sighed, the failure sinking into the pit of her stomach.

"Or the guy."

"I didn't want the guy to begin with." The words hurt when they came out, as if her throat had been seared. Mattie dipped into her pint and withdrew a heaping scoop of ice cream, hoping the cold treat would salve the wounds inside, yet knowing even as she ate it that the calories would be nothing more than a temporary fix.

"Sure you did. I watched the show every night, too, girlfriend, and I saw how you looked at him."

"Hillary, he was a reporter. He was out to use me for a story, not fall in love with me." She curled deeper into Hillary's sofa, seeking comfort in the soft beige fabric. The blinds were drawn, foiling any possible spotting by the reporters. The amber light from the incandescent bulbs cast the room in a muted glow. Hillary's apartment, tastefully decorated in a clean, earthy style much like Hillary herself, had always felt comfortable, but was ten times more so today.

"Maybe David had a good reason," Hillary said.

Mattie arched a brow. "What good reason could there be?"

"You'll never know if you don't go back and ask him."

Mattie shook her head and dug into the container for more ice cream. A pint, she was afraid, wasn't going to be enough. "Nope, I'm not going back."

"Don't you have to, according to the contract you signed?"

That had been her plan earlier today—to return and finish the show as promised. But now, after David's betrayal, all she wanted to do was hole up and consume ten pounds of ice cream. "I think I have grounds to argue for fraud or something."

"Well, don't you *want* to, out of curiosity?" Hillary licked her spoon clean, then waved it in Mattie's direction. "All of Lawford is waiting for this cliffhanger, you know."

She wasn't waiting. She knew how it was going to end. She'd seen it all fall apart, in slow motion. Everything she'd thought had been perfect had shattered into a hundred pieces between the cole slaw and the French fries. She freed a piece of a cherry and popped it into her mouth. "Everyone is dying to know whether I'm going to fall in love—"

"Or fall apart."

Mattie drew herself up. "You know I won't."

"But the city doesn't know that. What better ending for this, and what better lesson for your girls, than to go back there, strong as steel, and face them all? If you run away, you look—"

"Weak and scared."

Hillary leaned forward, placing a gentle hand on Mattie's knee. "I wouldn't blame you if you were. But I think a big part of you wants to know how this ends, all the same."

"I can tell you one thing," Mattie said, diving again into the Cherry Garcia, "it won't be a happy ending."

"You've got a hell of a scoop, Bennett, what with this whole missing Average Jill thing and the public all wanting to know what really happened today," Carl crowed through his cell phone. "When are you turning in the story?"

"I'm not."

A long moment of silence hummed over the line.

"You're…what? Are you insane? This is your job, you do realize that, don't you?"

"I do. And I decided I don't want the job anymore, not if it means destroying someone else's life."

Carl snorted. "Since when did you grow a conscience?"

"Since the reporter became a part of the story." He drew in a breath, his gaze drifting over the manicured landscaping of the mansion. From his bedroom window, he could just see the edges of the garden, the tranquility of the koi pond. If he'd had any doubts, the sight of the dark, still water erased them, as had the long solo walk back to the mansion earlier. "I'm done, Carl."

"What are you going to do?"

David chuckled. "I don't know. Maybe write poetry for a living."

"Poetry? Are you insane? Doing drugs?"

"Nope. Just tired of writing unhappy endings. I want to see a few people go off into the sunset with smiles on their faces."

Carl let out a sigh that sounded like disgust, but, David hoped, it could have been regret over losing one of his reporters. "You really *are* crazy, Bennett. And a damned romantic. Have I told you how much I hate romantics?"

David laughed. "Many times."

"I told you, stories about average women with average lives don't sell papers."

"I know, Carl. That's why I quit. I can't give you what you want. Not with Mattie Grant's story and not with anyone else's. It's just not in me anymore."

He wanted more. Damn it all, he wanted the white picket fence, he wanted to be putting down grass seed every year and he knew who he wanted to be putting it down with. That was, if she didn't bury him in the backyard for what he'd done.

"Don't go getting ahead of yourself. What does sell papers is stories about average women falling in love with average men, despite all odds."

David grinned. "Carl, are you turning into a romantic on me?"

"Hell, no. It's just smart business. Have you seen the sales of romance novels, for Pete's sake?" On the other end, Carl tapped a pencil against his coffee cup, the ceramic mug making a gentle ding across the phone line. "You bring me one of those happy endings you're so damn hot to write and I'll publish it."

David thought of Mattie's exit from the diner, the betrayal on her face. He wasn't sure he'd be able to fix that, no matter how much he wanted to. "What if I don't have a happy ending with Mattie? Or what if I get really, once-in-a-million lucky and she picks my sorry bachelor self at the end of this, and neither one of us wants to be on page one?"

"Then find another one of those happy endings. I hear they're all over Lawford. That feel-good Friday section's been too sappy lately. Maybe you can jazz it up."

"Are you offering me a job, Carl?"

"I don't want to see you selling pencils on the street to support your poetry habit, dammit. So you better say yes."

David chuckled. "You know I never could resist a nice offer, Carl."

"I'm not nice and don't you go telling anybody I am. Now get me something by Monday morning or I'll forget I rehired you."

David hung up the phone. One corner of his life was neat and straight again. He looked out over the grounds of the mansion and saw Mattie walking along the garden path. Steve, bringing up the rear, was hurrying to catch up with her.

There was another corner of his life, possibly too hurt by the mess he'd created to ever be straightened again.

But nothing was going to stop him from trying, anyway.

Mattie ambled along the garden path, avoiding the mansion for now. Although she'd had Hillary drop her off at the side of the house, she hadn't quite committed to going back in there. So she'd stuck to walking the grounds, warring with herself over staying or going.

"Hey, Mattie, wait up!"

She pivoted and found Steve, huffing his way through a slow jog behind her.

"You came back," he managed between breaths.

"Yeah, but I'm not sure I'm staying," she said, trying in vain to ignore the stinging of unshed tears behind her eyes. She was mad at herself for wanting to cry, but most of all, mad that she'd believed David was someone she could trust and care about. "I'm done with this show. With people lying to me. With all of it."

"Don't leave, Mattie, not now."

"Why?" Her voice cracked a little. "Give me one good reason why."

"Because you might just fall in love." Steve smiled at her and for a moment, she saw another side of the producer. A human, softer side that didn't seem driven by the ratings game.

Mattie plucked a leaf off a tree and tore it into pieces. "None of these men is here for me. None of them knows who I really am. They're here for the money."

"Did you *let* them get to know you?"

"Of course I did."

"I dunno. I watched the tapes at the end of the day and I'd say you were a little…distant."

Had she been? She'd accused David of putting up walls, had she done the same thing? As her mind rocketed back over the past few days, she realized she had, indeed, kept her self to herself.

"Well, in the end it was better to be distant, wasn't it?" Mattie's gaze went to the lawn, right where the pretend soccer field had been. It seemed a million years since she'd kicked that topiary ball at David and set in motion something she hadn't expected.

Feelings she hadn't counted on.

"Are you talking about David?"

"Yeah."

"He came back, you know," Steve said. "He's here, in the mansion."

"You didn't kick him off?"

Steve let out a laugh. "What and mess with the ratings I'm going to get by having the two of you in the same room again tonight?"

She chuckled. "I should have known it would all come down to the show in the end."

He shrugged, a slight sheen of red filling his cheeks. "Sort of. In a way, though, you've changed me. I watched you out there," he said, gesturing toward the lawn. "You aren't afraid of anything. Not afraid of what people might think of you, not afraid of going after what you want—"

"Me? I'm afraid of more than you think."

"Well, no one would know it." He cleared his throat and rubbed the back of his neck. "Anyway, you did a great thing for me."

"I did?"

"You got me to kick the death sticks."

"Cigarettes?"

"Hell, no. I'm dumb, but not stupid. I don't smoke. I eat fast food." He grinned and held up a paper container filled with julienned carrots. "I kicked the French fries. Went cold turkey yesterday, watching that basketball game. Figured maybe this time next year I can go one-on-one with you." He grinned. "Might make good TV."

She laughed. "Always thinking of ratings, aren't you?"

"Hey, if I could turn kicking my junk food habit into a TV special, I would." He paused a minute, a hand on his chin. "Say…"

"Don't even think about it," Mattie said. "Steve, you have to draw the line somewhere."

He waved a hand at her. "I'm a TV producer. I don't have a line to draw."

"Then I'll send you some chalk."

He laughed. "Deal. I'll keep my diet off the Lawford Channel Ten airwaves, if you get out there and choose yourself a man tonight." He glanced at his watch. "We go live in the next fifteen minutes, so if you could get inside and get ready now, I'd *really* appreciate it."

"What if I don't?"

"That's your choice. It'll probably give me a heart attack *and* get me fired, but I'll understand." Steve grabbed a carrot stick and munched for a second before continuing. "I think if you don't go tonight, though, you're always going to wonder why David did what he did." He wagged the remaining half of his carrot stick at her. "And if there's anything I've learned about you in these last few days, it's that you follow through on everything you start."

He gave her an awkward nod, as if he'd considered a hug but changed his mind, then left her alone in the garden.

Mattie considered Steve's words. Follow through on this? This wasn't like chasing a ball down a field or blocking an aggressive midfielder. This was more than her shins or her elbows. It was her heart. And this time the pain was ten times more than anything she'd ever sustained on a field.

Worse, there wasn't an Ace bandage or a cast to take care of it. There was only time. And time, as Steve had just reminded her, was something she didn't have the luxury of. Not tonight.

She ambled down the path and circled the koi pond, pausing at the edge and bending down to greet the bright-orange fish. They poked their noses at the surface, probably hoping for food.

"Sorry, guys. I'm empty." She spread her hands to prove the words. Everything about her felt empty right now, as if David's betrayal had sucked something out of her, leaving part of her on the speckled table of the diner.

"Mattie?"

She didn't turn around at the sound of David's voice. Instead, she stayed where she was, studying the koi as if they were the only things she could manage right now.

"Mattie, I'm sorry."

She twirled a finger in the water. Two fish came up to see if her digits were edible, then disappeared again in the inky darkness of the pond. "I don't want to hear your explanation. I don't even want to talk to you right now."

"Please, Mattie. Just give me a minute. You don't understand. I was a different man before I met you."

She stood and pivoted toward him. "David, I don't flatter myself that I'm so hot that men become completely different creatures just by meeting me. That's not how it works with a girl like me."

"What do you mean, a girl like you?"

She got to her feet and swung over to the semicircular bench. "I'm a soccer player. I wear cleats and ponytails and I only put on makeup when there's a banquet. I am not what anyone would call a dream girl."

"I've dated those made-up women," David said, rising and moving to the bench with her. "My dream is not a woman who can wear the right thing but not have a decent conversation with me. It's not a woman who cares more about herself than other people. It's you, Mattie. You are it."

"I'm your *story*. I'm your dream of a big headline."

"You *were* my story. You stopped being it the minute you swung that backpack over your shoulder and stomped out of the room, refusing to play by anybody's rules."

"Yeah, right. What kind of scoop are you trying to get now? And why on earth should I believe you?"

"Because I'm asking you to." He took a step forward and met her gaze. She wanted to trust what she saw in those blue eyes, but…she couldn't. "Listen, I'm telling you the truth now. My real name is David Bennett. I'm a reporter for the *Lawford Sun*. And I'm not going to write one damned word about you."

She looked away, blinked back the tears that threatened, then brought her gaze back to his, hardening herself against his words. "How do I know you aren't lying to me right now?"

He took her hands in his. His palms were warm and strong, the same palms that had held hers during the mutiny dance in the ballroom, the same hands that had clasped her with security at the top of the Tower of Chance.

But were they really the same hands? She'd thought they were, in the diner, and then found out they didn't belong to the real David Simpson at all.

"You're going to have to trust me," he said.

She closed her eyes for a moment, then opened them

again and jerked her hands out of his, her heart as heavy as the stones that ringed the pond. "I don't know if I can do that, David."

Chapter Eleven

Mattie stood outside the closed ballroom doors, this time clad in her own clothes, the same outfit she'd worn when she first showed up at the James Estate, Lands' End backpack slung over her shoulder, running shoes on her feet, flip flops in the pack along with one memento from the show—the Hermès scarf.

"Honey, you can't wear that! You're about to pick the man of your dreams," Salt said, grabbing her by the hand and dragging her into the makeshift dressing room the show had created in the parlor.

"I can and I will," Mattie said. "I don't want to wear anything out of that closet." Nor did she want to go into that ballroom, but she would. For her league. After smoothing things over with the producer, he'd told her she could still get the fifty thousand if she did this final episode. She could make it through the next few minutes for the girls. She'd think of them and not herself or how her heart felt as if it had been through a meat grinder.

Salt ignored her and rummaged among the ball gowns, emerging with a long, pink sparkly thing with spaghetti straps. "Come on, what about this one?"

Mattie shook her head. "Nope."

Pepper, who stood to the right of the closet, reached in and yanked a blue one off the silver rod. "This one?"

"I told you, I'm not wearing any of those clothes ever again."

Pepper looked stricken, his black spiky hair seeming to droop a bit. "But Steve will have my hide if you don't wear one of these outfits."

"This show is called *Love and the Average Jill* and I intend to be the average girl for once."

"But—"

"This is who I am, guys," Mattie said, spreading her arms. "It's always who I've been."

Salt's mouth turned down. Pepper, however, brightened and gave her a pat on the back. "Good for you for being yourself, honey. Not many women are brave enough to go out there without their Prada."

Mattie laughed. "To me, it takes courage to put *on* the Prada."

Salt threw up his hands in defeat. "Well, honey, at least let me put some waterproof mascara on you first."

"Waterproof mascara?"

He grinned and withdrew a pink tube from his makeup bag. "It's the beauty secret of reality TV stars everywhere, honey. You get to look beautiful, even as you're crying your eyes out."

Mattie hoped she'd keep the tears in check. She'd had to swallow back the hurt of David's betrayal a thousand times since she'd come back to the mansion. Each time it seemed to get harder, not easier. "Load me up, Salt. I think I'm going to need a lot of that stuff tonight."

Bowden stood on the steps of the mansion and started his argument anew with the stone-faced butler. "You have to let me talk to her. I have to give her this package."

"No one gets in to see Miss Grant." The man stood there, clearly not about to budge.

Bowden let out a sigh. He couldn't let Mattie throw everything away, especially not the happy ending he was sure she had within her reach. On last night's episode, he'd seen the way she looked at David—not to mention the way he looked at her—and knew those two were meant for each other.

At first when he'd seen the special newscast today and found out who David Simpson really was, he'd been ready to march over here and tear a hole in the man's heart for messing with Mattie. But then he'd done a little research of his own. Bowden had discovered the reporter had started out writing stories that sent many bad guys to jail, uncovering facts that helped the cops send the creeps away.

Then his career had morphed into something less noble and it seemed David Bennett had lost track of who he was.

Until he'd met Mattie Grant. Bowden smiled. She had a way of changing the people she met, that was for sure.

"You have to let me give her this," Bowden said, holding up the envelope. Inside were all the old articles of David's that he'd found on the Internet. Surely she'd see David wasn't the selfish fiend the news had made him out to be.

"No." The butler raised his chin. "I will not. You may speak to Miss Grant at another time."

Then he shut the door in Bowden's face. From the other side, he could hear the sound of a lock turning.

Bowden slumped onto the granite steps and turned the envelope over and over in his palm. He was going to have to let Fate take her hand with what happened inside that mansion tonight.

He could only hope and pray Fate had been watching Lawford Channel Ten all week and seen, as he had, that Mattie Grant and David Bennett were definitely made for each other.

Mattie stood in the ballroom in her sneakers, feeling oddly at home. Maybe it was being in her own clothes. Maybe it was the relief that it was finally going to be over. Or maybe it was just the calm before the storm.

She was in the center of the room, surrounded by the cameras, the four remaining bachelors, the camera crew, a teary Pepper and Salt, Larissa and Steve. She flicked on the battery pack for her microphone and braced herself for one more public display of her private life. Soon, she'd go back to being just Mattie Grant, soccer league chairman and coach, and leave behind Mattie Grant, bachelorette with love on her mind.

Somehow that sounded sad. She glanced at David, then looked away before she could change her mind about what she had to do.

Larissa came around to the center of the room, cast a sympathetic look Mattie's way, then turned toward the cameras. Tweedledee counted down, then gave her a signal to begin. "For this, our special live finale, Mattie will be choosing the winning bachelor. Will it be love in the end for the Average Jill? Or heartbreak for the bachelors who are sent home?"

Larissa took a step back, then waved a hand toward Mattie. "And now, I give you our bachelorette, Mattie Grant."

Mattie cleared her throat and stepped forward, her nerves a swarming mess in her stomach. She looked at each of the men in turn, trying to listen to the confusing jumble in her heart. That day at the diner, David had told her to trust him, to feel what was real and tangible in her gut.

And yet he'd been lying to her.

She had to choose a final bachelor. Someone. By doing so she would fulfill the terms of the show and get the fifty thousand dollars she needed for the league. She didn't have to fall in love.

And she hadn't, had she?

But as the pain ripped through her heart anew, she wondered who the real liar in the room was.

Mattie closed her eyes, drew in a deep breath and whispered out the name. "Jim."

Larissa let out a gasp. Even Jim said something that sounded like "Really?"

When she felt she could stand it, Mattie finally opened her eyes. And saw nothing. The lights had gone out.

"What the hell?" Steve shouted. "This show is live, you know! Someone fix this now!"

"Mattie." David's voice, soft and quiet, before her.

"David?" She thought of turning away, of bolting from the room, but remembered her vow to Hillary. No one would see her weak or scared. Especially herself.

"I didn't have a scarf on me, so this was the next best thing."

"You did this?"

"It's my trust walk, Mattie. I only have a few seconds before someone figures out how to get that power back on. Tripping a GFI isn't foolproof. But it buys me a little time."

"What do you think you're doing? I told you—"

"I want you to listen to my voice, nothing else. Don't look at anyone or anything, just listen to me."

She shook her head, trying not to listen, yet wanting to at the same time. Her memory brought back a kaleidoscope of images from the past week: the moments at the koi pond, the soccer game, the walk in the gardens.

Had some of it been real? Had she been wrong? And if she didn't listen to him now, would she always regret it? "But—"

"And don't 'but' me, either." He chuckled. "I meant what I said about being a different man before I met you. Remember how I told you about that T-shirt warehouse? Well, I was the one who wrote that story about the drug smuggling operation."

"You were?"

"It's what got me the job with Carl, my editor. I've been there ever since." He drew in a breath and took her hands in his. In the dark, his touch felt firmer, larger. In the background, she could hear Steve cursing and running around the various rooms of the mansion, trying to find a way to get the lights back on. "But no one knows why I went into the business of uncovering lies."

Between them, she could almost feel the layers of David falling away, the chunks in the walls they'd each built breaking apart. In the dark, there was nothing separating them anymore, and she allowed a tiny crack to open in her heart. "Why did you?"

"I grew up in a house filled with them," he said quietly. "My mother cheated on my father, my father cheated on my mother. Each of them had me, their only child, keep the other's secrets. I suppose—" he let the word out on a sigh "—that some psychologist would say I couldn't do anything about the lies in my own house, so I worked on uncovering everyone else's."

"I think that's a perfectly valid reason to go into the

field you did." She felt empathy for him, knowing what it was like to have that kind of childhood. She understood his search for something that could restore what he had lost.

"Maybe it was, when I started, but every time I did one of those stories, I lost a little piece of myself. And then, when a story came along that deserved to be done, like the one on your league, I'd rush through it to jump ahead to the juicier headline."

"*You* wrote that article?"

"That was me, the lazy and shoddy one."

"I'm sorry, I didn't know—"

"No, you were right. It's who I became. And I thought I was proud of the job I did. Until I met you."

"I didn't do anything special, David."

He reached up and cupped her face, his grasp seeming to encompass all of her in the dark. "Ah, but you did, Mattie Grant. You were too good. There's no way you're average. You're out-of-the-ballpark special. And you made me believe there were good people in this world again."

She'd thought she'd come on this show to change the lives of the girls in her league. To start the teams up again, to see the girls achieve their dreams. She'd had no plans to impact anyone else's life. And yet, here was David, telling her that simply by being herself, she had changed him.

Just by being an average woman. By not being what everyone else in her life had always tried to get her to be—something other than herself.

"And so," he went on, "I quit my job."

"You quit? You aren't reporting on what happens between us?"

"Nope." She knew, even without seeing his face, that he was wearing that familiar grin, the same one she'd seen the first day he'd challenged her.

She echoed that grin with one of her own. "So I could, ah, do anything I wanted to you right now and no one would see it?"

"Yep. The cameras are, essentially, blind."

"What about you?" she asked, stepping into the circle of his arms. She noted how perfectly she fit, as if she were meant to be in this space. "How are you seeing?"

"I can see perfectly," he whispered. "I see the woman I'm meant to be with, the one who brings out the best in me, who makes me want to be a better man. Who makes me want to be more than I even knew I could be."

"I did all that?"

"You and that topiary ball," he teased. "You are one tough competitor."

She grinned. "We all have to be good at something."

"And is there anything else you're good at, Matilda?"

Hearing her given name spoken with his deep, sexy growl was the last straw. She swallowed her doubts and went with her instincts. So many times on the field, her gut had served as her barometer, telling her when to act, when to hold back. She'd never doubted it there—why doubt it now when she was making one of the most important decisions in her life?

"There's a lot I'm good at," she whispered, and leaned forward to kiss him. In his lips she found the truth she'd been seeking. And everything else that had been missing in her own life, too. David Bennett wasn't the only one who'd been changed by the *Average Jill* experience.

His hands tangled in her hair, lifting it and caressing the back of her neck. She arched against him, moving her palms up his back. Everything about David felt solid and firm. Dependable.

She pressed her body to his, grateful for the dark, yet wishing they were anywhere but in a ballroom surrounded by other people and a muttering, panicked producer scrambling to find a working light switch. She wanted David, and only him.

David's kiss deepened and Mattie groaned, opening her mouth more to his, her tongue dancing with his, tasting and teasing, as they explored more of each other.

And then, just when things were getting good, the lights came back on, casting them both in the public glare. They broke apart, blinking in the sudden brightness.

"Well, damn," Kenny said, an irritated frown on his face. "If I'd known all I had to do was kiss like Valentino to win this, I'd have stepped up to the plate a long time ago. Women love my kisses." He sent a smile Larissa's way. "Want to try it out?"

She gave him a horrified shake of her head.

"You don't know what you're missing." Kenny shrugged.

Steve had a knowing grin on his face, as if this were exactly the ending he was planning, not to mention the one that would garner the best ratings of all time for Lawford Channel Ten. But for David it wasn't over, not yet. The lights were on—which fit neatly into his final plan.

He turned away from the human audience, ignored the virtual one lurking behind the cameras' eyes and refocused all of his attention on Mattie. "I know you've already made your bachelor choice tonight, but I'd like to up my ante and ask you to reconsider."

She cocked her head. "Up your ante? I thought you already did that with, ah, what we were doing in the dark."

He grinned. "That was just my opening stake." He took both her hands in his and locked his gaze with a pair of emerald eyes that saw parts of him no one else ever had. "I love you, Mattie Grant."

"You…you…" Her eyes grew wide, her breath hitched.

"What, you don't have a ready play to send back at me?"

"I hadn't expected *that* kind of corner kick tonight."

"This is reality TV. Surprises are part of the game." He grinned, delighting in the look of joy lighting up her face. "But I would have told you whether there were cameras here or not. Because I'm going to love you long after the commercial break."

She laughed. "You better. Because I'm going to make you work to keep your ratings, David Bennett."

He wrapped his arms around her waist and drew her closer to him. "Oh, yeah? How do you intend to do that?"

"By loving you right back." She placed a quick kiss on his lips.

"Hey," Jim said, striding forward, "she picked me, not you. Get the hell out of here. Let *me* confess my love and all that stuff so I can get my money."

"Sorry, Jim, but Mattie's not going to be a bachelorette much longer." David released her and lowered himself to one knee, withdrawing the ring he'd bought earlier that evening when he'd still been praying that she would forgive him. He flipped open the dark-blue velvet box and turned the marquis-cut diamond toward Mattie. She gasped and her eyes shone with unshed tears. "I believe I owe you a poem."

She nodded, her fingers at her lips. "You do indeed, Shakespeare."

He cleared his throat. "Okay. Here goes. 'I'm not much of a rhymer, but I'm trying to beat the TV timer, and tell you I think—you're the prettiest woman in pink, I have ever had the pleasure to see.

"'Marry me, Mattie Grant. And together we'll plant, the seeds of a new life, with you as my beautiful wife…and bury those damned cameras at sea.'"

She laughed long and hard. "You want us to play on the same team? Forever?"

"Forever and ever." He took her left hand in his and held the ring at the end of her ring finger, waiting. "That doesn't mean we can't go one-on-one once in a while, too."

"In that case—" her smile widened and she slid the ring onto her finger "—I say yes."

Steve let out a whoop and Larissa burst into tears. Jim scowled. "Hey, now you get to split the big bucks with her. Did you just do that for the cash?" he said to David.

"Nope. My half of the prize money is being donated to the Lawford Girls' Soccer League for new fields, uniforms and to start a fund for college scholarships for the girls." He looked at Mattie. "That is, as long as the chair accepts my donation."

"Oh, I do." She smiled. "Every last cent."

"Well, what do I get for being in second place?" Jim asked.

"Actually," Steve said, coming up and draping an arm over Jim's shoulder, "how about *Love and the Average Jim*?"

Jim considered that for a minute, a hand on his chin. "I can live with that. And the fifteen beauties you're going to get me." He grinned, nodding, clearly liking the idea more and more.

Steve caught Mattie's gaze over Jim's head. "Well, I think we might put a twist or two into the sequel. We learned a few lessons here."

As the two men walked away, the cameras moved in on Mattie and David for the closing shot. Mattie reached behind David's back, flicked the battery pack for his microphone off, then did the same with her own. Then she whispered the new rules for the game ahead.

Judging by the smile on her husband-to-be's face, there wasn't going to be a need for a referee.

Epilogue

Bowden Hartman sat in the break room at Speedy Delivery Services and watched the update of the *Love and the Average Jill* show. Who knew a little envelope mischief could end up with a wedding *and* a sequel?

Well, he'd known. He hadn't known Mattie would choose David Bennett, of course. That had been serendipity's doing, but this ending was even better than he'd predicted. Not to mention how *Survival of the Fittest* had turned out. While Miss Indiana had never become an outdoorsy girl, she had won over most of the male competitors, resulting in her being the sole survivor at the end of the show. She'd netted a *Sports Illustrated* swimsuit issue gig out of it and the fifty thousand dollars, which she promptly spent on a day at the spa, detoxifying and exfoliating and removing all evidence of her time spent away from a mall.

"Mattie and David Bennett are rumored to be honeymooning in California," the Lawford Channel Ten newscaster said, "which is hosting the Women's World Cup Soccer Tournament again this fall." She then turned to Larissa for commentary.

"They wouldn't confirm or deny the report that they were venturing out West after their hush-hush wedding," Larissa Peterson said to the cameras, then cupped a hand around her mouth, "and frankly we don't blame them."

Bowden chuckled. One happy ending down. He looked at the stack of packages and envelopes waiting in the crates designated for his route today and decided it was time to create another one.

* * * * *

SILHOUETTE *Romance*®

Matilda Grant signed on to a reality
show to win fifty thousand dollars,
but once she met contestant
David Simpson all the rules changed!

Don't miss a moment of

The Dating Game

by

SHIRLEY JUMP

Silhouette Romance #1795

**On sale
December 2005!**

Only from Silhouette Books!

Visit Silhouette Books at www.eHarlequin.com   SRRTDG

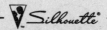

SPECIAL EDITION™

**Here comes the bride…
matchmaking down the aisle!**

HIS MOTHER'S WEDDING
by **Judy Duarte**

When private investigator Rico Garcia
arrived to visit his recently engaged
mother, the last thing on his mind was
becoming involved with her
wedding planner.

But his matchmaker of a mom
had other ideas!

*Available January
wherever you buy books.*

Where love comes alive™

Visit Silhouette Books at www.eHarlequin.com   SSEHMW

eHARLEQUIN.com

The Ultimate Destination for Women's Fiction

Visit eHarlequin.com's Bookstore today for today's most popular books at great prices.

- An extensive selection of romance books by top authors!

- Choose our convenient "bill me" option. No credit card required.

- New releases, Themed Collections and hard-to-find backlist.

- A sneak peek at upcoming books.

- Check out book excerpts, book summaries and Reader Recommendations from other members and post your own too.

- Find out what everybody's reading in Bestsellers.

- Save BIG with everyday discounts and exclusive online offers!

- Our Category Legend will help you select reading that's exactly right for you!

- Visit our Bargain Outlet often for huge savings and special offers!

- Sweepstakes offers. Enter for your chance to win special prizes, autographed books and more.

Your purchases are 100% guaranteed—so shop online at www.eHarlequin.com today!

INTBB104R

If you enjoyed what you just read,
then we've got an offer you can't resist!

Take 2 bestselling
love stories FREE!

Plus get a FREE surprise gift!

Clip this page and mail it to **Silhouette Reader Service**™

IN U.S.A.
3010 Walden Ave.
P.O. Box 1867
Buffalo, N.Y. 14240-1867

IN CANADA
P.O. Box 609
Fort Erie, Ontario
L2A 5X3

YES! Please send me 2 free Silhouette Romance® novels and my free surprise gift. After receiving them, if I don't wish to receive anymore, I can return the shipping statement marked cancel. If I don't cancel, I will receive 4 brand-new novels every month, before they're available in stores! In the U.S.A., bill me at the bargain price of $3.57 plus 25¢ shipping and handling per book and applicable sales tax, if any*. In Canada, bill me at the bargain price of $4.05 plus 25¢ shipping and handling per book and applicable taxes**. That's the complete price and a savings of at least 10% off the cover prices—what a great deal! I understand that accepting the 2 free books and gift places me under no obligation ever to buy any books. I can always return a shipment and cancel at any time. Even if I never buy another book from Silhouette, the 2 free books and gift are mine to keep forever.

210 SDN DZ7L
310 SDN DZ7M

Name	(PLEASE PRINT)	
Address	Apt.#	
City	State/Prov.	Zip/Postal Code

Not valid to current Silhouette Romance® subscribers.

Want to try two free books from another series?
Call 1-800-873-8635 or visit www.morefreebooks.com.

* Terms and prices subject to change without notice. Sales tax applicable in N.Y.
** Canadian residents will be charged applicable provincial taxes and GST.
  All orders subject to approval. Offer limited to one per household.
  ® are registered trademarks owned and used by the trademark owner and or its licensee.

SROM04R   ©2004 Harlequin Enterprises Limited

SILHOUETTE *Romance*

COMING NEXT MONTH

#1798 LOVE'S NINE LIVES—Cara Colter and Cassidy Caron
PerPETually Yours
Justin West wasn't looking for commitment, but everything about
Bridget Daisy exemplified commitment—especially her large
tabby cat, who seemed to think there was room for only one
male in Bridget's life. Justin couldn't agree more. So he vowed
to be a perfect gentleman. Only problem was he had *never* been
a gentleman....

#1799 THAT TOUCH OF PINK—Teresa Southwick
Buy-a-Guy
Uncertain how to help her daughter win a wilderness survival badge,
Abby Walsh buys ex-soldier Riley Dixon at a charity bachelor
auction. But will their camping trip earn Abby's *romantic* survival
skills merely a badge for courage, or a family man to keep?

#1800 SOMETIMES WHEN WE KISS—Linda Goodnight
Family business might have brought Jackson Kane home after
ten long years but it had always been personal between him and
Shannon Wyoming. Now he was her key to holding on to all that
she held most dear...but what price would she pay for saying
"yes" to his proposal?

#1801 THE RANCHER'S REDEMPTION—Elise Mayr
Desperate to save her sick daughter, widow Kaya Cunningham had no
choice but to return to the Diamond C Ranch and throw herself on the
mercy of her brother-in-law. And though Joshua had every reason to
despise Kaya for the secret she'd kept from his family, his eyes reflected
an entirely different emotion....

SRCNM1205